The Oregon Incident

Children of the Wild, Volume 5

Prudence MacLeod

Published by Prudence MacLeod, 2024.

The Oregon Incident
(second edition)
By
Prudence MacLeod
Copyright, June 28/2017

Assignment

The director sighed and looked at the earnest young woman in his office. To say she was beautiful would do her a disservice. Even in plain work clothes this girl was stunning. "Special Agent Larise Parker, how did you ever end up here?"

"It's a long story, Director Bridger," she sighed, as she sank into a chair. "Suffice it to say, here I am. I'm told you have a special team to investigate the bizarre and unusual. I'd like a shot at it if an opening comes up."

"So I've heard." He gazed at her for a long moment. "Why is that?"

"Truth is, sir, I'm sick of humans."

"Yeah, it can sour you when your partner turns on you, that's for sure. You do understand some of the work you're looking for is dangerous."

"I do." Again he looked at the file on his desk, tearing his eyes away from her. "Sir, I'm no fool, I know Director Compton chose me for this department for my ass, not my assets, but I can do the job, I can. Please, just give me a chance to be useful."

"Useful?"

"Director Bridger, the purpose of this department is to safeguard the nation from threats both foreign and domestic. I believe in that mandate, I have the skills, I can do this job."

"All right, Agent Parker, here's the thing. Sometimes, we in this department encounter some things that humans should never have to deal with. Now, I have one assignment and one only available right now, and I don't have a spare agent to put on it."

"I'll take it."

"I haven't told you what it is yet," he grinned. "Larise, this is probably just a wild goose chase, nothing more, but in case it isn't, don't try to be a hero. You go, you investigate, you assess, and if, in your professional judgment, action needs to be taken, contact me. Understood?"

"Sir ..."

"Think of this as a test case. Your record shows that you all too often take the initiative when you should wait for back-up. Don't do that, not on my teams. The thing is, Agent Parker, at this level shit can get out of hand at light speed, and nobody plays solo. It's far too dangerous."

"Understood."

"All right, Agent Parker, you're on your way to Oregon. Here's the case file."

She gave it a cursory glance then looked up. "Seriously? You're sending me out to hunt for Bigfoot?"

"No, Agent Parker, I'm sending you out to discover why half the people who do go looking for Bigfoot never come back. That town, Whitbourne, was evacuated overnight and not one soul has ever spoken a single word of sense about it, nor have the eighty plus deaths that happened at that time been satisfactorily explained. Now there's fresh murders in that area.

"Your mission is to investigate, record, and report. Look, I believe you have the tools for this job, now I need to know you can follow instructions, and that I can trust you. Prove up on this and you'll I'll make sure your place here is solid. Deal?"

"You can count on me, sir."

"Go book a plane ticket, Agent Parker."

───── ⟨⟩ ─────

BATTERED AND TERRIFIED, Larise Parker stumbled down the overgrown forest road, gasping for breath. She reached the encampment where she'd been staying, but there was no help to be found there.

"Hapoble! Hapoble mon ile pedo!"

"Where were you? Did you enter the god's sanctuary? Did you? Were you within the place that is forbidden? Grab her, we'll use her for the sacrifice. Grab her."

Stones and other objects were sent her way, some scoring hits and others, misses. Now she was fleeing from her former companions. She continued to run until she stumbled and fell headlong over a steep embankment. At her scream, her pursuers turned back and joined the chanting, as the gathered people began to pray for forgiveness and the blessings of the forest god.

At the bottom of a rough slide, the battered woman regained consciousness. Summoning all her reserves, she managed to regain her feet and struggle onward. It was near dawn the next day when she reached the highway, and hours later before she was picked up by a passing motorist who took her to the nearest hospital.

ONCE AGAIN, THE VAMPIRE king was holding court in the great hall. He was speaking, but his queen reached out to grip his arm, bringing him to an instant silence. She turned to a powerfully built man sitting near her. "You're about to get a phone call, Terry. I have a sense we need ..." His phone began to buzz. Terry Sawchuk, once the government's go-to secret agent, and now chief agent of the vampire king, looked to the big man at the head of the table.

The king nodded and Terry pulled out his phone. "It's Egan Bridger," he said, then answered the call. "Director Bridger, good to hear from you. What's up?"

"We've got some weird shit happening, Terry. Your sort of thing."

"I'm listening."

"Ever hear of Whitbourne, Oregon?"

"Nope. What's its claim to fame?"

"It's deserted, has been for over sixty years."

"Deserted?"

"Yes, the whole damn town fled within the space of a few days. Nobody could ever make any sense of it. Anyway, in the past few months things have been happening out there."

"Things?"

"Strange things. A bunch of pagan nut jobs are claiming the old god has returned to the forest. They've set up a camp a few miles from Whitbourne, but refuse to let anyone get past them. They say that town is sacred to the god.

"So, for years now, hunters, Bigfoot seekers, hikers, and whatever else who got near that place just disappeared, never to return. It started getting more frequent recently and thus came to the attention of my department. A few days ago a woman came out of those woods, nearly dead, and babbling insanely about what had happened to her."

"The worshipers smoking some Oregon Gold up in the hills?"

"She's one of my agents, Terry, young and ambitious, but the makings of a good agent. Terry, I don't have the people to put on this. I thought you might be interested in having a look."

Terry glanced to see the queen nodding and the king agreeing. "All right, Egan, I'll take a look at it for you."

"Terry, they're tightening the budget ..."

"Three-fifty each, per day, for a six-person crew, plus expenses."

"Seriously? I must have done something right in a past life."

"It's okay, Egan. I'll pad the hell out of the expenses."

"Fair enough," laughed the director. "What else will you need?"

"Just the usual, badges for the crew, everything you've got on the case, and I want one of my people to interview that agent."

"Not a problem, Terry, but it won't help you. She's crazy as a loon and makes no sense at all. It's a damn shame, really."

"Okay, send me what you've got, and I'll hit the road in the morning. That woman in the hospital?"

"Oh yes."

"Send me a location. She'll be my first stop."

A WOMAN IN A STRAIGHT-jacket sat staring at the walls. She was getting irritable and panicky as the medication began to wear off. Voices sounded outside her door, and she strained to listen. "Has she been taken off all medication?"

"Yes. She should be awake now, but I warn you, Agent West. She makes no sense and gets frustrated, almost violent when you can't understand her."

"I'll speak with her alone. Terry, make sure there are no prying eyes or ears."

"Yes, ma'am, I'm on it."

A few moments later, the door to her room opened and a tall elegant woman entered. Something about this woman exuded power and command. The girl in the straight-jacket didn't move. "Hello, I'm Ella West. I'm going to take that restraint off you now. Do you understand?"

Suddenly the prisoner came alive. She leaped to her feet, begging the tall woman with her eyes as she implored her with inane babble. *"Be silent."* The woman froze and trembled with unreasoning fear. Ella West, the eldest of the vampires, took the girl by the shoulders and gazed into her eyes.

"You've been under a vampire's compulsion before," mused Ella. *"Listen carefully, you are at peace. You have full control of your emotions and your thought processes. English is your native language. When you speak to me you will use English. Do you understand?"*

A wave of peace swept over the distraught woman. The panic left her eyes and reason returned. "Yes, ma'am, I understand."

"Very good. I'll remove that restraint now, you no longer need it," said Ella. She took off the straight jacket, then sat on the edge of the bed and gently pulled the woman down beside her. "Let's start again. I'm Ella West."

"Larise, Larise Parker, Special Agent Larise Parker. Oh gods, I can't thank you enough for that. I've got to report. I've got to warn them ..."

"That's what we're doing now, Larise. I'm part of a special team assigned to the case you were working on. Tell me, are you feeling up to it now?"

"Yes, yes, I am, thank you."

"Then come, I'll take you to the agent in charge. He'll connect you with Director Bridger." She rose to her feet and led the way out of the padded cell. A wide-eyed psychiatrist watched as the mad woman walked away. There was a man waiting for them at the end of the corridor. "Larise, this man is Terry Sawchuk. Terry is in command of our team. Terry, Larise has experienced something quite unusual. I think perhaps she should be assigned to us."

"Ella?"

"Your decision, Terry, but I have a strong feeling about this."

"Okay, if you're sure. Come with me, ladies, we'll use the doctor's office for a few minutes. You don't mind, do you, Doc?"

"Knock yourself out," said the bemused psychiatrist.

They closed the office door then sat down. Terry took out his phone and called.

"Bridger."

"Egan, it's Terry. Look, I've got your agent here with me and she's fine now. Egan, I'd like to have her assigned to my team for this exercise."

"Ah dammit, Terry, tell me you're not going to rob me of another agent."

"Maybe, not sure just yet," chuckled Terry. "So, do I get her for the mission?"

"First tell me how you managed to bring her around, if you actually did manage that."

"They did, sir," said Larise.

"Agent Parker, are you seriously all right?"

"Good as new, Director Bridger."

"How???"

"It's a very old technique, Director," said Ella. "I'm Ella West, and I've had experience with this sort of thing before. The reason we want Agent Parker with us is twofold. She has firsthand knowledge of the incident, and I'd like to keep an eye on her condition for a few days. I highly doubt there'll be any more trouble for her, but I want to be certain."

"Ella West, you're that special consultant who worked with Terry on the serial killer case a few years ago."

"Yes, Director, that is correct."

"All right, I can't see any problem with it. Agent Parker, you are now assigned to Terry Sawchuk as liaison for the duration of this case. You will report to him and get your orders from there. Get to it people, there's been another killing in that area. An agent will meet you at the Portland airport with your equipment and rental vehicles." With that he was gone, and Terry put the phone back in his pocket.

"Are you ready for action now, Larise?"

"I am, sir."

"Terry, call me Terry. We'll pick up the rest of the team, then you can bring us all up to speed at the same time. Let's go."

They walked outside where a helicopter was waiting for them. They climbed inside, then it lifted off. As they cleared the city, Ella turned to Larise. *"Larise, you have now joined a unique and highly skilled team. You will trust them, and you will be loyal to them. In the coming days you will see many unusual things. You will accept these things as normal, but*

you will never speak of them to anyone except members of the team. Do
you understand?"

"I understand."

"Relax and be at peace with us, Larise. We'll keep you safe." She
visibly relaxed and Ella patted her hand then turned to gaze out the
window.

Eventually, Larise saw what looked like a castle below, and then
the chopper began to descend. She was led into the great hall and
introduced to the king and his court. "Are you ready for some questions
now, Agent Parker?" asked Terry.

"Yes, of course."

"Start at the beginning, tell us what happened to you," said the
king, a big and powerfully built man who exuded command.

"I was assigned to look into the troubles being reported in Oregon.
There is a town there called Whitbourne that was suddenly deserted
about sixty years ago. Dozens of people were killed there at that time.
There are rumors of murders, strange disappearances starting up again,
and a group of wannabe pagans have suddenly begun to block all access
to that area."

"Wannabe pagans?"

"I did a quick study of neo-pagan groups in the US," replied Larise.
"Those people in the mountains aren't doing anything I recognize as
legit, but they are true believers. They believe some old god of the forest
has returned and made them his chosen people. They say the deserted
town is sacred to him and no human is allowed to go there.

"I found them and managed to join the group, waiting for a chance
to slip away unnoticed. I made it to the abandoned town early one
morning. It looks like everybody just stopped what they were doing
and ran away. Spooky as hell, especially on a foggy morning.

"I spent most of the day poking around, looking for something,
anything, to give me a clue as to what was going on there. All I found
was moldy houses, rusty cars, and ghosts, until late in the afternoon.

"I came out of a house to see a bull elk staring at me. It looked unhappy. I started to back away then it began to change. It reared up on its hind legs and began to make angry sounds. The more it changed into a vague man-like form, the more the sounds began to sound like language. The thing still had the elk's head and back hooves, legs and a tail, but also the torso of a man with huge clawed hands, and it grew fangs.

"It bellowed at me and charged. I put several bullets into it, but that just made it angrier. I fought, but it tossed me around like a rag doll. I rolled with the punches as best I could, but it kept coming, bellowing at me the whole time.

"I thought I was done for, but the rage seemed to drive it to complete madness and it began to thrash at trees with its antlers, tear at the ground with its hooves, and I ran before it turned its attention back to me.

"I could hear it in my mind as I ran, still shouting at me in that strange language. I don't know if it followed me or not. I was pretty beat up, and when I made it back to the camp I tried to ask for help, but they couldn't understand me. They started throwing stones at me, trying to catch me, and I fled.

"Eventually I made it to the highway where a nice old man in a pick-up truck stopped for me. He couldn't understand me either, but he did take me to a hospital. They patched me up, found my ID then contacted the police. I tried so hard to make them understand, but they jumped me and I ended up drugged, in a straight jacket, and being shipped back to New York. The rest you know."

The king nodded thoughtfully for a moment then spoke to Ella. "Mother, why did you insist Agent Parker be brought to us?"

"When I approached her, she began to plead with me. Her words would be completely unintelligible to anyone else but me or perhaps Torvil. To anyone else it would just be mad ramblings, but it was an ancient tongue. Sire, she was under some form of compulsion, but I've never seen anything like it before.

"I was able to override it and restore Larise, but I was concerned that, should she ever come under the care of people with skills like Amanda or Clyde, it could all unravel again. Harald, I don't think we dare risk this with a government agent."

"I agree, Ella," sighed the king. "You did right, people."

"Are you going to kill me?" asked Larise.

The king chuckled at that. "No, Agent Parker, we would like to keep you on our payroll instead of the government's for a while, at least until our people have time to help you completely unravel what happened to you. Agent Parker, you're working with us now and we will protect you."

"Protect me, from what?"

"Whatever it was that attacked you, to begin with. Our people will now proceed to deal with whatever that was, and they are uniquely equipped to do that.

"All right, Terry, choose your team and go."

"Actually, Sire, I don't think I should lead this team."

"Terry?"

"I work best in urban settings, Sire. This is pure deep woods and high mountains. This is a job for Igor."

At that, one of the young men sitting at the long table looked up and grinned. The pretty woman beside him nudged him with her elbow and winked. The king smiled. "Looks like you're up, Igor. Terry, do you have all the information for him?"

"I do, Sire."

"Very well then, Igor, Terry's contracted for a six-person team. Choose your people."

The young man grinned with delight. "I'll need the Lady Hawk, of course. I'll also need Kylie."

"Me?" asked a tall dark woman as she arched an eyebrow at him. "Why me?"

"You're an urban tracker, the best in the world. I'll need you to find some people who once lived in the empty town. I'll also need you to write up the pretty reports for the Director when we're finished. I'll make the reports for the king." The woman smiled and nodded.

"I'll also need Miss Ella. She has knowledge of what's happened to Miss Larise, and can help her if things go crazy."

The king nodded his approval at this. "As they all too often do in these cases. Who else?"

"We have promised Miss Larise protection. I'll take Branimir."

A tall athletic man in his early twenties suddenly looked up. "Me?" He was grinning from ear to ear. Since Larise walked into the room he hadn't taken his eyes off her.

"Da, you. You're her bodyguard. Keep her safe, Bran, above all else, keep her safe."

"I will, Igor, I swear it." He stood and came around the table to stand behind her chair. She spun to look up at him and he winked at her then turned his attention to the room. She looked back as the king spoke.

"You have your team, Igor. Gudrun is due back later this afternoon. Eric can take you wherever you want to be dropped off."

"I believe there is a man waiting for us in Portland, Sire," replied Igor. "Eric will need to get some sleep. We should leave in the morning. Come, people, gather what you'll need then rest. We leave at dawn." With that, Igor rose, saluted the king, then left the room, his team following close behind.

Prepare

Larise was shown to a well-appointed room and Branimir followed her in. She turned to him with wide eyes and took a defensive stance. "Listen, friend, I'm trained in martial arts and there's no way in hell I'm sharing this room with you, so get that grin off your face and get the hell out."

His posture was completely relaxed as he gave her a shy smile then stepped past her to drop the spare blanket from the bed onto the floor near the door. "This will do nicely."

"You're not sleeping there, not in this room."

"I have to," he replied with a sloppy grin as he put his back to the wall and slid easily down to sit on the blanket, "I'm your bodyguard. Igor said to keep you safe, to protect you, and so I must."

"I don't give a shit what Igor says."

"I do. Igor says stay near, keep you safe, and so this I will do."

"So, what, Igor's your slave master?"

Branimir tilted his head and gave her a quizzical look. "He is the alpha."

"The alpha? What the hell does that mean?" Larise felt like she was slipping away into a mad world again. No, she had to gain control of her thoughts, stay focused, understand fully what was happening.

He sighed deeply and tapped his head back against the wall. "You don't know, do you? You don't know, and therefore you don't understand. Ah well." With a startling animal grace he rose to his feet, stepped out of his shoes and tossed off his t-shirt.

"What the hell do you think you're doing?" Larise had taken a step back and assumed a defensive stance as he reached for his belt. She nearly screamed as he dropped his jeans to the floor then shimmered into a huge wolf. With her hand over her mouth, she stood staring at him, but he made no move at all.

Larise had seen wolves before, none like this. He was too big, and there was something else different about him. The wolf sat grinning at her for a few moments then shimmered back into the man, pulled on the jeans and shirt, then sat back down, leaning his shoulders against the wall. Larise swallowed hard then sat on the edge of the bed. She could feel the vampire's compulsion fighting and overriding the terror. "Okay, that was scary. What the hell are you?"

"Werewolf. Igor is our pack alpha," said Branimir. "Igor says protect you, and protect you I will."

"So, you obey him instantly? You could challenge for dominance; wolves do that don't they?"

"Challenge Igor? Are you crazy, woman? I have no wish to die. To challenge Igor would be certain death. Let me tell you something about us. When we were young, a number of us were captured and held prisoner, tortured, trained as assassins. Those who didn't please the masters were thrown to hungry fighting dogs, killed. Several died this way.

"Igor was thrown to the dogs three times and each time he killed all the dogs and climbed back out of the pit. He was our alpha there as there were no adults. He protected us, fought for us, used his wits to keep us alive. Igor's our alpha, and I'll run with his pack to my dying day. I'm here to protect you and that I will do. Let us not talk of this further."

His utter devotion to his leader was clear, and somehow comforting. This strong young man, this powerful werewolf, would guard her with his life, and since they were going back to that insane place in the mountains, that was a good thing. He wasn't staying so close to hurt her, he was just protecting her.

"Okay, got it, I'm sorry. I'll try to stop being so defensive. I'm a really private person, not used to sharing a room, but I'll try."

"Someone you trusted hurt you," he said, his voice gentle and filled with compassion. "That won't happen with me."

She nodded slowly. "What kind of wolf are you? I've seen wolves before, but none like you."

He grinned at that. "Mr. Torvil says we're dire wolves, an old type of wolf that no longer exists in this world."

"Except for you guys?"

"Da, except for us."

"Can I see it again? Maybe if I get used to seeing it you won't scare the bejesus out of me when you change."

He chuckled and rose to his feet, shed his clothes, then shimmered back into the wolf. He sat down and gazed at her, his tongue lolling out. She almost laughed; he looked so silly. At that point another woman entered the room.

"Hi, I'm Elaine. I've brought you some tea and snacks. If you need anything at all just call me. I'm number one on that list above the phone." She turned and spotted the blanket on the floor. "Branimir, if you shed all over that blanket there will be repercussions. You stay off that and I'll bring you something more comfortable to sleep on."

The wolf whimpered and nudged at her, but she turned away, a twinkle in her eye. "No, you're not allowed to shed on the good blankets. You know better." She grinned and winked mischievously at Larise.

He whimpered and lay down, rolling onto his back. "No, I'm not rubbing your belly, you've been bad." He wagged his tail and whimpered again, trying to look cute. She laughed and bent to scratch his belly, bringing a groan of delight. "Oh yeah? You like that, don't you?" Another groan of delight. "Are you going to wait for me to bring you a proper bed?" Again he wagged his tail and groaned.

Elaine rose, smiling. "So, Bran's your bodyguard, Miss Parker. You're a lucky woman, ma'am. He's the best." She turned back to the wolf who was blocking her way out of the room. "What? Oh no." The wolf didn't move so she sighed and turned back, winked at Larise again, then took one of the tiny sandwiches from the platter and tossed it over her shoulder. He caught it easily.

She saw the look Larise gave her and smiled. "Ma'am, the werewolves are a gentle, loving, people, playful, full of mischief and fun. They're intensely loyal and protective. They're also highly intelligent and utterly savage when aroused. You could ask for no better protector. Don't be afraid of him."

"He'd kill me if Igor told him to."

"Igor would never give that order," replied Elaine.

"You seem pretty sure of that."

"I'm utterly certain. Forgive me, ma'am, but you need to prepare for your mission. With your permission, I'll go now, but if you need anything just call."

Larise watched her go then noticed the wolf was back in human form. He was watching her with interest, and yet a look of compassion on his face. "What?"

His question surprised her. "How do we gain your trust, your loyalty, pretty woman? Your paranoia is deep, and you don't trust. I think you want to trust, but something inside stops you."

"You're right about that," she sighed as she sat back on the bed. "I trusted the wrong man once and got hurt badly. When I first went into police work I trusted my partner, damn near got me killed. The son of a bitch was on the take."

He didn't speak, just nodded that he understood. "Why is this so important to you?" she asked.

"We go to a strange place to face an unknown enemy. All on the team are known to each other, all trust each other fully, we know each other well."

"All except me."

"All except you."

"And I don't really know any of you, or anything about you. I can't just blindly trust, I can't. I'll tell you this, I'll do my job to the best of my ability, and I'll be loyal to the team within the confines of my job. Will this satisfy you for now?"

He nodded and then Elaine returned. She laid a padded bed on the floor for him. "There now isn't that better? Give me the blanket now." He passed her the blanket and she laid it back on the bed. With a smile she excused herself and vanished through the door. A few moments later she tapped on Igor's door, then passed him the small recording devise Branimir had slipped to her as he returned the blanket.

Ella and Kylie were in the room with Ronni and Igor. Together they listened to the recording. "The girl's still tormented," sighed Ronni. "Your compulsion is holding her together, Ella, but she's struggling. I'd say her trust issues are deep and go back a long way."

"I agree," replied Ella. "There's more I must tell you all now. I have no idea at all what she encountered, but I have a suspicion and it concerns me. She spoke to me in an ancient language as I entered her room in the institution. It startled me, as I haven't heard that language spoken since well before Mobutu was made."

"What did she say?" asked Kylie.

"She asked for help, begged me to believe her. I sensed a compulsion at work on her, a compulsion poorly executed. Something had tried to reorganize her mind to speak only that language. I managed to override it, but not eradicate it. It's still at work in her subconscious.

"I truly need to work more with her, but I'm afraid I'll frighten her too much if I try. First, she needs to learn about compulsion, what it does and is capable of. Only then can she make the decision to ask me for the help she needs.

"Setting Branimir as her bodyguard was wise, Igor. If anyone can gain her trust, he will."

"Ella, you said you have a suspicion about what she encountered," said Ronni. "Can you share that suspicion with us?"

"Yes, and I believe that you, Ronni, as the royal veterinarian, will have greater insights to its nature than the rest of us."

"Me? How so?"

"Dr. Rhonda Stockman, don't play the innocent little girl with me," chided Ella, shaking a finger at Ronni. "Your knowledge of, and studies into, animal behavior will be invaluable here. You see, when Mobutu came to New York to challenge me, I don't think that was his first trip to these lands."

"Ella?"

"No, Kylie, I now believe he was here before. You see, that language Larise spoke was the language of his people at the time he was made vampire. She described how the elk changed into a partial human, much like the vampires change into the half cat."

"Oh shit," said Igor. "You think Mobutu tried to make an elk into a vampire?"

"Deliberately or not, that's what I think happened. Igor, when we face this thing, I must be the one to fight it, kill it."

He nodded his agreement. "Great Mother, perhaps you should share this with the king. If Queen Sally is willing, she may be able to confirm your suspicion for us."

"I believe you're right, Igor; Sally's insights could be invaluable to us. Come, Kylie, let's see if the king and Queen are still awake."

She rose gracefully and offered her hand to her lover. She and Kylie left hand in hand. Igor sat silently gazing at the screen before him. Finally, Ronni nudged him. "Hey there tall dark and furry, pay attention to your wife."

With a soft chuckle he put his arm around her shoulders. "This is the information for the case, my pretty bird. It's mostly just her reports of the town, the people, and here she reports on the people camping, praying to the creature. She managed to infiltrate their group and observed some strange behavior.

"Here we have the Director's notes. He, too, was concerned about her growing paranoia. I think we need to watch her closely."

"You don't trust her? You think she'd betray us?"

"Not deliberately, sweet lady, but this is one messed up woman. Poor Bran has a hard task before him."

"You mean because he has the hots for her?"

"Da, that."

"Honey, what would happen if she rejects him?"

"He will let her go. It's not our nature to force such a thing. However, he'll try for her, he can't help himself. Sweet Ronni, I have an extra task for you on this mission. I need you to watch Bran's back."

Rhonda sighed and stroked the hair back from his brow. "What's going through that head of yours, my love?"

Igor pulled her close and kissed her cheek. "I fear he may instinctively trust her and she not be worthy of that trust."

"And if he senses you keeping an eye on them it could make him think you don't have confidence in him to do his job. I'll watch her for you, lover." He smiled and kissed her cheek again then went back to studying the screen.

Ronni stood, walked around to face him, then tossed aside her clothes and put her hands on her hips. Igor chuckled as he closed the laptop and rose to take her in his arms. "All work and no play make Igor a dull boy?"

"All work and no play make Ronni a cranky girl," she replied. "Stop fooling around and kiss me like you mean it."

Later, as he lay sleeping beside her, Rhonda Stockman, the immortal Lady Hawk, sighed and lightly stroked the hair back from his face. "I'll be watching your back too, my big bad wolf. I'll be watching your back too."

Heading West

Larise awakened slowly, barely breathing as she took in as much of the room as she could see. As the memories of where she was returned she began to relax, then froze as a male voice spoke softly. "Awake I see, did you sleep well?"

He was there, by the window, watching the sunrise. "Yes, I did, did you?" she asked as she sat up and tousled her hair.

"I did, yes."

"Why don't I believe you?"

"No, I did, truly. We're perfectly safe here in the castle. Once we leave, I will sleep lightly, but here it was safe to sleep."

"If it's so damn safe here, why did you insist on being in the room with me? Oh, I get it, to keep an eye on me. You're not just my bodyguard, you're my jailer as well." She stiffened and pulled the sheet close around her body.

"There's that paranoia again," he sighed, relaxing back against the windowsill. "No, Larise, I'm not your jailer. We have no fear of you exploring the castle; if we had another day I'd be happy to show it to you myself." He turned to give her that gentle smile. "I insisted on being in the room with you so you'd become more comfortable with me in your space. When we rest tonight we'll be in a strange place, you'll sleep more lightly, and I want you to feel safe with me so close by."

She sat up and gazed at him, studying him. At first glance she saw a hardened athlete, yet a seemingly gentle man. However, she'd seen the wolf and had an idea of what he could become, what he might be capable of. For some reason she wasn't totally freaked out. It must have to do with the treatment that woman, Ella West, had given her. Still, her natural wariness was asserting itself, causing her to withdraw.

"Fine," she said, "but you're not watching me get dressed."

He chuckled at that. "I'll wait outside the door until you're ready. We'll have breakfast together then join the team at the hangar."

She watched as he left the room. This man, this werewolf, who'd become her bodyguard, moved with the ease and grace of a warrior. The sight of him stirred something inside, but with a shake of her head she let it go and padded to the bathroom. There was no time for that sort of thing now, it only brought pain in the end anyway. A few short minutes later, she appeared with her overnight bag in hand.

"Toss your bag on the bed, Elaine will see it gets to the plane for you."

"I'll keep it handy, if you don't mind." She sighed and began to admonish herself. *"Dammit, Larise, get over yourself."*

"Keep it close if you wish, come." He gently took the case from her hand, then led the way to the dining room where there was a large buffet style breakfast.

She watched as he chose a large plate of ham and eggs, toast, and coffee. Branimir saw her looking at his plate as she ate her cereal. "What?"

"Nothing."

"Woman, if you say a single word about kibble, I'll ..."

"No, no, I wasn't ..." Larise was laughing and he shook a finger at her. He grinned and returned his attention to his plate.

She was relaxing with him at last. Larise studied him as he ate, admiring the powerful sweep of his shoulders, the strong hands, and the easy gentle manner that exuded from him. In another time and place she'd have had no problem getting closer to him.

They finished eating and rose from the table. Suddenly she was nearly in a panic. "My bag, it's gone. It was right here and now it's gone."

"It's okay," said Branimir, "it's okay. Charles took it. It'll be waiting for you at the plane. Come on, Igor and Dr. Ronni will already be there."

"Charles? Who the hell is Charles?"

"He's the butler. So, in the case of the missing travel case, the butler did it in the dining room." That made her laugh again. In spite of herself, Larise was starting to like having this big bad wolf at her side all the time.

They hurried outside and to the hangar. He'd been right. Igor and the pretty blonde were already waiting for them. Larise noticed her bag with three others and a pile of gear.

"Good morning, Agent Parker. Did you sleep well?" asked Igor.

"I did, in spite of the wolf in the room."

"Oh, does he snore?" asked Ronni.

"Terribly," she replied, a twinkle in her eye.

"Hey now, there'll be none of that," said Branimir, shaking that finger at her again.

Larise turned to Ronni. "So, you're a doctor?"

"I'm a veterinarian," she replied. "Dr. Rhonda Stockman, at your service. Call me Ronni."

"Larise. A vet, well that makes sense, considering what these guys are. Are you a werewolf too?"

"Nope, I just married one," grinned Rhonda.

Just then Ella and Kylie arrived. "Perhaps, in a gesture of good faith and trust, Larise should know who and what we all are," said Ella. "What do you think, Igor?"

"Da, we ask for her trust, then we should show trust," he replied. "Agent Parker, you know both Bran and I are wolves. My beloved Ronni is a werehawk, Miss Kylie is a human like you, but she is the best urban tracker in the business."

"I know who Kylie Green is, we studied her methods at the academy. So, who or what are you, Doctor West. You quelled the madness in my mind, how did you do that? Are you a magic Geni?"

Igor stepped in front of Ella protectively. "When you speak to the Great Mother, keep respect in your voice. Miss Ella is vampire, the oldest and most powerful of all the vampires. She is the most dangerous person on this planet, and she is the king's champion. When we face the creature that attacked you, it will be she who kills it."

Larise looked past him skeptically. Her skepticism turned to fear as Ella extended her fangs and let her eyes change. Suddenly, with a swift movement she tossed aside her dress and shimmered into the saber-toothed tiger. The beast was huge with massively muscled front quarters and foot long fangs. The cat shook itself then gave a coughing growl.

Instinctively, Larise had leaped back into Branimir's arms as Ella changed into the cat. With wide eyes she watched as Kylie scooped up Ella's dress and patted the cat. The tiger morphed back into the woman and Kylie wrapped the dress around her again then kissed her cheek. Without a word Ella gracefully climbed onto the plane.

Larise turned to Branimir and realized she was snuggled in his arms, worse yet, it felt far too good. She put her hands against his chest, and with a mischievous wink, he released her. Blushing, she turned and boarded the plane.

As the plane rose into the air Ella sensed Larise's eyes on her. She turned and smiled. "I know, not what you expected a vampire to change into. However, it was the long-toothed cat that made me what I am. Cat, not bat. Of all the vampires, only I can fully become the cat that made us what we are. The others only half change. They grow taller and more muscular with longer arms, sharp claws, and cat like faces with long fangs."

Larise swallowed hard then spoke. "Can you tell me what you did to help me?"

"It is a gift known only to the vampires. We call it the compulsion. If a vampire uses the voice of command, a human will obey. No one can deny the compulsion. I believe that what happened to you, Larise, was a crude form of the compulsion. My compulsion is the strongest, and so I was able to override the other."

Larise was quiet for a moment while she absorbed this bit of information. "So, you're saying that thing I fought was a vampire?"

"In a manner of speaking, yes. Most vampires are created from humans and so we can live among you successfully as long as we can control the madness."

"The madness?"

"The thirst for blood, the mad desire to kill. That burning thirst, that desire to kill, is ever present for the vampire. Those who have the strength of will to control it can live forever, unseen, unknown," said Ella.

"And those who can't?"

"I hunt and destroy them utterly," replied Ella, a hard edge creeping into her voice. "Larise, I believe that a maddened vampire came to this land and, for some reason, tried to make a vampire of an animal. That language you were speaking was of his childhood. What he managed to create was an abomination. It's crude attempt to compel you caused you to speak his language."

"Oh my god, so are you going to hunt that vampire too?"

"I have already done so, and destroyed him utterly. Now I find myself still cleaning up the mess he made."

Larise sat back, trying to absorb everything she'd been told. "Wow. So you used this voice of command to help me. When this is over are you going to use it to make me forget all about you people?"

"That depends. If you remain with us then no, I will leave your memories intact. If you decide to return to your old life, then yes, I'll remove certain memories from you."

"That makes sense. So, the reason I'm not totally freaked out by all this is because you prepared me with that compulsion thing."

Ella smiled. "I did give you a little nudge in the right direction."

Larise smiled. "Did you make me put up with my bodyguard?"

"No, girl," grinned Ella. "You're on your own with the big bad wolf."

"Miss Ella," groaned Branimir, "you're not helping." Ella winked at Larise and patted his arm.

The plane landed in a remote section of the airport where another government agent was waiting for them. "Which one of you is Sawchuk?"

It was Kylie who answered. "Jamie, what the heck are you doing out here on the west coast?"

"Kylie? I disagreed with the former director and got busted down. So, where's your boss?"

"He's on another case. This is Igor Wolf; he's leading this team."

"If you say so. Good to see you back in action, Agent Parker. This is yours, Agent Wolf." He passed a briefcase to Igor. "Your badges and ID are all there. I assume Kylie will fill in the blanks. Here's the keys to the vehicles, two four-wheel drives. You'll be staying in Tanner's Ridge, I take it."

Igor just accepted the keys from his hand and didn't speak. "Right, need to know. Okay folks, have fun playing with Bigfoot. I've got three days off and I'm headed for the beach." With that he turned and walked away.

They watched until he drove away then Igor tossed one set of keys to Larise. "You've been here before, lead us to the nearest town with a decent hotel or motel with wi-fi where Kylie can work. We'll go from there."

"That'll be Tanner's Ridge," she replied. "There's a comfortable motel there, and it's the nearest town to Whitbourne. I stayed there before. Shall I call ahead and book rooms?"

"Da, three rooms, at least one with wi-fi. Do you have weapons?"

"Weapons?"

"Weapons," replied Igor. "Are you carrying a gun, knives, anything at all?"

Larise gave him a questioning look. "I assumed I was on conditional return to work. Am I to be trusted with a gun?"

"You are. Bran, get her weapons and arm yourself. Kylie?"

"Already packing, boss," grinned Kylie.

"Then let's go."

Branimir passed Larise a sidearm and shoulder holster then strapped one on himself. He tossed the rest of their bags into the back seat of the vehicle then got in. He noticed her smiling at him. "What?"

Larise grinned as she drove away with the rest of the team following in the second car. "Oh, I was just trying to picture you trying to get out of that harness and then get your clothes off to change into the wolf. Could be tricky in an emergency."

"Oh, no problem," he replied, "I can manage."

She saw his smile and thought again how easy it would be to get used to having him around. "Right, so what aren't you telling me?"

"Okay, I'll talk. When a shapeshifter changes, their clothes fall away. I could change into the wolf in mid leap and the clothes would just fall down to the ground. We usually choose clothes that are easy to get back on in a hurry, not because we need to get out of them quickly.

"The vampires now, they're different, all except the Great Mother. They only partly change so they need stretchy or lose fitting clothes."

"I'm curious," said Larise. "Why is she called the Great Mother?"

"Miss Ella was the first vampire. All other vampires came from her or her descendants. She is the original."

"Wow. Do you know how old she really is?"

He smiled as he spoke. Larise saw and realized this man worshiped the old vampire. "Da, she still has a dagger made from the tooth of the cat that changed her into what she is. It was carbon dated at one point three million years old."

"Wow. Seriously? So, she's immortal. She's pretty special to you too, isn't she?"

"Yeah, she is. It was she who made the king what he is, she who took Igor from the death camp, then returned with him to protect us all while the king and his men killed our keepers and brought us out.

"I have a good life, and it is because of her. Igor kept us alive, but it was the Great Mother who helped us override our training to become ourselves again. She did the same for you."

"The compulsion?"

"Yes. I still have all the memories, and the skills I learned in that camp, but they no longer rule me. Thanks to Miss Ella, I now rule them.

"Now, tell me about Larise Parker. How did such a pretty woman end up as a special agent?"

"Me? Well, okay, my dad was a policeman and I wanted to be just like him, to make him proud. Thing is, police work isn't what I thought it'd be. I wasn't fighting crime or helping people, I was assigned to vice and spent far too long trying to entrap men looking for prostitutes. I got sick of it and applied to the FBI.

"I was successful, but shortly after that I was picked up for the special teams. I knew at the time that it was my looks that got me transferred, not my skills. Anyway, the result is, here I am, going back toward my worst nightmare and hanging out with werewolves and vampires."

"Is that so bad?"

"It's starting to grow on me," she smiled.

"That's good to hear. I'm starting to enjoy hanging out with you too."

WHILE RONNI DROVE, Igor turned to speak with Kylie and Ella. "Kylie, see if you can find me someone who lived in that town when it was abandoned. I'm curious why it was abandoned so suddenly. If it was a single beast coming on the scene the men would hunt it. Even if it came back from the lands beyond, it would take a long time for the process to unfold.

"Some people would leave, later others, and later still more. Why did they all leave at once?"

"I've been wondering that myself," replied Kylie. "It couldn't have been a mass killing frenzy by a vampire, because there would have been reports of a serial killer or mass murderer, but there's nothing. I can't find anything at all about what happened there. Guess I'll have to go deeper, hack into a few secret government systems, that sort of thing."

"My thoughts as well," said Igor. "Miss Ella, can you tell me why you wanted Larise with us? In truth I would rather have had Clara and asked for a mobile lab. I wanted Bran to help me scout out the place."

"Forgive me, Igor," replied Ella, "I should have taken you into my confidence sooner. I can't tell you how I know for certain, but I strongly believe she is still connected to that creature somehow. Her cautious nature has been converted to near paranoia by her contact with it. Her wariness and insecurity are as akin to the natural instincts of a prey animal as you can get.

"Beyond that, she is pulled back to this place by her contact with the carue. Carue is an ancient name for a crazed animal, an animal that drinks blood. We dared not leave her unobserved, for if she returned and was then apprehended by her own people, a skilled psychiatrist could easily unravel the truth of our existence.

"Besides that, I have no real idea of the extent of her contact with it, of what she might become if that contact was too strong."

Igor nodded as he absorbed this information. "Da, I understand. You had no chance to tell me before the king said to choose my people. Had I known I would never have assigned Bran to be her bodyguard, I'd have chosen a vampire instead. He needs to be warned."

"I agree, Igor," said Ella. "I'll make a pretense of giving her another session so you can take him aside and warn him. Also, you might want to change his mandate a bit."

"Oh yeah, that I will do."

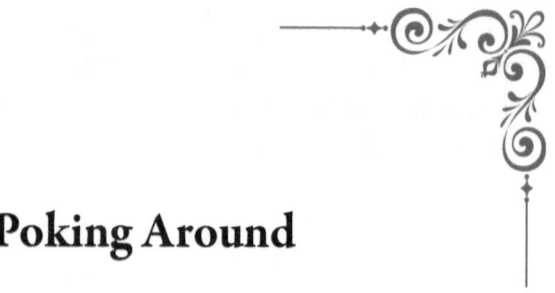

Poking Around

They arrived at the motel and checked in. Ella took Larise aside for another session and Branimir helped Igor unload the gear. Ella carefully sat Larise with her back to them so she wouldn't see them talking.

"What are you saying to me, Igor?"

"I'm saying you must protect her, yes, but watch your back as well. Bran, if she starts to turn, protect yourself first. I mean it, protect yourself above all else. We don't truly know what she is or might become. The great mother brought her along because it was too dangerous to leave her in the hands of the humans.

"Bran, protect yourself, here, as well," said Igor, as he lightly touched his friend over the heart. "We don't know what she is, what she may become."

"Da, I will, Igor. Why is it never easy?"

Igor chuckled at that. "I don't know, but it never seems to be. Bran, if anything happens to me ..."

"I know, Igor. We will look to the Lady Hawk for guidance. I'm the next strongest, all will trust me in this."

"Then I'm at peace with it. You go collect Larise and then the three of us will go talk to the local police." As Branimir fetched Larise, Ronni gave Igor a questioning look. He glanced at the sky and she nodded.

They boarded a car and Larise drove to the sheriff's office in the next town. As the vehicle left the parking lot the hawk leaped skyward. Kylie set to work at her computer while Ella kept her eye on the hawk soaring lazily above. Any shift in that slow circle to the right would alert her to danger.

AS THEY ENTERED THE sheriff's office, a tall deputy pulled his feet from the desk and stood to greet them. "Agent Parker, is that you?"

"The one and only," replied Larise.

"Oh my, just look at you, all cleaned up, speaking English, and everything. You're not even wearing that pretty jacket with the strings that tie in the back."

"Nope, I'm good to go."

"Girl, I don't even want to know what you were smoking that day," said the deputy, shaking his head. "So, what are you doing back here?"

"A new team's been assigned to the Whitbourne case. I'm just along as adviser and observer. Agent Wolf here is in charge of the investigation."

"Agent Wolf."

"Deputy."

"What can I do for you, Agent Wolf?"

"There was another killing in the area of Whitbourne a few days ago. What can you tell me about that?"

"Not a damn thing," replied the deputy.

"How about I show you this badge and ask you again?" said Igor, flipping open his new ID.

"Holy shit, is that real?"

"It is. So, I ask you again, what can you tell me about the recent killing?"

"Okay, well, there's not a lot to tell. The body was found near where those freaks were camped."

"Were camped?" asked Larise. "You mean the so-called acolytes of the old god who inhabits Whitbourne?"

"Yeah," replied the deputy, "them. We got a call about a dead body and when we got there they were gone. The body had been torn apart, a woman, about thirty, brown hair and eyes, five-five, dead about twenty-four hours by the time we got there. She looked to be one of those characters, had no ID on her or nothing. That's about all we've got on it, Agent Wolf."

"Thanks," replied Igor, as he made a note in his book then returned it to his pocket. "Deputy, do you know of anyone who lived in that town before it was abandoned?"

"My granddad," he replied. "You can find him across the street in that cafe, playing chess with, and losing to, the gal who owns the place. He won't talk about it though."

"Mind if I ask anyway?"

"Be my guest, Agent Wolf. Hey, before you go, just what are you people investigating here, and to what purpose?"

Igor gave him an easy grin. "There's weird shit going on up there, weird and dangerous. Our job is to figure out what it is, what causes it, and if possible, make it stop."

"And then bury the truth so no one ever finds out, right?" asked the deputy.

"That decision comes from higher up than me," replied Igor, "but, yeah, probably."

"It figures," said the deputy, as he resumed his seat. "Good luck with Gramps." He returned his feet to the desktop as they filed out.

As they left and crossed the street to the cafe Larise spoke to Igor. "Why did you tell him that?"

"Tell who what?" asked Igor.

"The deputy, why did you tell him we'd bury the truth of what we find?"

"Because we will," he replied, "but more, it was what he wanted to hear. I easily confirmed his suspicions about big government, and made him see me as a friend, a regular guy, all at the same time. He was quite forthcoming with us, and that confirmed for him that he was right to be so. In his mind now we're just like him, doing our job, drawing our pay, and waiting for the few days off we get at the end of a case."

She gave him a thoughtful look. "There's more to you than meets the eye, Agent Wolf."

"Told you," grinned Branimir, as he stepped closer and put an arm over her shoulders. For some reason she left it there.

As they entered the cafe there were two people playing chess in a corner booth. The woman rose to serve them, and the old man sat back to wait for her return. "He's all yours, Bran," said Igor, "go get him." Branimir nodded, and then, with an easy smile, ambled over and sat down across the chess board from the old man.

The old fellow looked up as Bran reset the pieces. "She'll be a while," he said easily. "I'll set it back for you when I leave."

"Who the hell are you, and what do you want?"

"I'm a seeker of knowledge," replied Branimir. "I search for the odd and unusual, as well as for the downright scary and nasty. I search for the unknown and dangerous." He moved a chess piece and the old man glanced at the board then made a move.

"Okay, so you're either hunting for Bigfoot, or you're one of them writers. Why come to me, I got nothing of interest for you?"

Branimir moved another piece on the board then spoke. "Long ago you lived in the town of Whitbourne. For some reason it was suddenly abandoned, and all the people disappeared. No one would talk of why.

"Recently a friend of mine made her way to that town. She was found days later, beaten, traumatized, and babbling in some unknown language. When she regained her command of English she told me a strange and unbelievable tale."

"Really?" The old fellow made another move on the board.

Branimir grinned and made a swift move. "Yup."

"And you tell me this because?"

Branimir paused for a moment to ponder his next move. At last he moved and then took up the conversation. "You used to live there. I'd like to know what you experienced, what made you leave."

"I'm old, can't remember a damn thing about it."

"Bullshit. When you age, the long-term memory holds true, it's the new stuff you lose. You remember all too clearly what happened up there, and it still scares the daylights out of you. I can sense the fear from you, I did as soon as I spoke the name of the town."

The old man made a move on the board then looked up angrily. "Just who or what the hell are you?"

"Believe it or not, I'm a friend," replied Branimir, as he made another move. "Check."

The old fellow's eyes snapped back to the chess board. He thought for a moment then made a move. "A friend, huh. So, just what are you here for, friend?"

"Bran, my name is Bran. Look, I already know something unusual happened back then. I know something strange happened to my friend a few days ago. I also have an idea that a bull elk is involved."

The old man blanched at that. He swallowed hard then met Branimir's eyes. His terror was real, but the gentle compassion and supreme confidence radiated by this strange young man calmed him.

"My friend, I know you're scared," said Bran, "but you have nothing to fear from me. Me and my people specialize in dealing with these sorts of things. We plan to find out what's going on up there and we mean to make it stop.

"No one need ever know you spoke to me. A young fool came in with stupid questions, but you just beat him at chess, and he went away mad. That's all."

"So I'm going to beat you at chess, am I?"

"Oh hell no," grinned Bran.

"That's what you think, you young pup. All right, but this stays quiet. I don't want to end up in the funny farm like that young agent last week, understand?"

"Understood."

"It started with the gas, at least that's what they said it was, volcanic gases, but there was something more in that greenish fog. Animals went crazy, people started to babble, making no sense at all. Within a couple of days the preacher said Satan had come, bloody bodies started turning up, and more people went crazy.

"When that big bull elk went nuts and started changing into a man everybody freaked out. Some shot at him but that only pissed him off. A scar faced man stood by, laughing, and talking to it in that crazy language. Everybody fled. A few folks tried to talk about it, but they wound up getting shock treatments. I was still a kid. I kept my mouth shut and my head down."

"You're a smart man, my friend. You say the man had a scar on his face?" The old man nodded. Branimir made a move on the board.

Seeing the move the old man pounced, snatching the piece away as he made his move. "Check, mate in three."

Bran studied the board for a moment then nodded his head. "You're too good for me, sir. Still, I wish we could have had a conversation at least."

"Sorry, I got nothing to say."

"So I see. Well then, have a nice day." Branimir rose and walked out, winking at Igor as he passed.

"What the hell was that about?" asked Larise.

"The old man would talk to Bran, and he has," Igor replied softly. "Finish your coffee now and we'll go find out what he said."

THEY WERE BACK IN THE car and returning to Tanner's Ridge. "Learn anything good, Bran?" asked Igor.

"Da, confirmed some and learned more weird stuff. First, the old man said there was a scar faced man involved. Miss Ella suspects her old enemy, Mobutu. She has described him as a man with a scar on his face.

"He also confirmed the bull elk partially changing into a man, but there was more. He spoke of a greenish gas. They were told at the time that it was volcanic gas, but I have to wonder."

"Yeah, green shit, as Terry would say. Ah well, with luck Kylie can find us more folk to interview."

"Why not just hunt down and kill the elk?" asked Larise.

"That's only one part of our job," replied Igor. "Yes. We have to deal with that, but we also have to find out what happened there, what else has happened in the meantime, and tie off any loose ends. Who knows how many more that elk has managed to infect, both animal and human?"

"Okay, I get that. We have to make sure there's no trace left that would point to a non-human, right?"

"Right," agreed Igor. "Tell me, do you think you could sense when that thing is near?"

Larise looked startled. "What? No. Jesus, what made you say that?"

"Just wondering," replied Igor. "Any of us can sense when danger is near, and we can sense when another were-wolf is close by. I just wondered if it was the same for you."

"Sorry, can't help you there," she replied.

There was something in her voice when she spoke, both Branimir and Igor caught it. Bran sighed and his shoulders sagged in disappointment.

They arrived back at the motel to find Kylie hard at work. She passed a sheet of paper to Igor. "There's a few addresses of folks who once lived in Whitbourne. Sadly, most are in nursing homes. The last three on the list are still on the loose though."

"I've already spoken with this one," said Branimir, as he reached over to tap a name on the paper.

"All right," said Igor, "take Larise with you and check out the other two. I think I'll go for a drive up that mountain road. Miss Ella, Sweet Ronni, you're with me."

They watched as Larise drove away, then Igor led the two women back into the room. Puzzled, Kylie looked up and Igor grinned. "Ladies, we may have a problem on our hands. Miss Larise is still connected to that creature. She denied it when I asked if she could sense it, but both Bran and I could smell the lie on her.

"Also, Bran spoke with an old man who was there when the town was abandoned. The old man told him there was a green fog and a laughing man with a scar on his face, shouting in that strange language while the elk/man killed the people of the town."

"Mobutu," sighed Ella.

"I believe so, Great Mother. I believe your suspicions were correct. What troubles me most is that Larise lied about sensing the creature. As I understand it, all vampires can sense the nearness of another vampire, especially the one who made them. The fact she can sense it concerns me as much as the fact that she lied about it."

"And so you sent her away with Branimir," said Ella. "That was good thinking, Igor."

"You've also got another problem, Igor," said Kylie. "The sheriff has been snooping around here for days, so the cleaning lady told me. He's trying to convince everyone that the recent woman's death was a suicide."

"Why would he do that?" asked Igor.

"Why indeed," agreed Ronni. "I took a scout around the town but saw nothing unusual. I'd actually like to do a fly over Whitbourne, see what I could see."

"Not just yet, my pretty bird," said Igor. "I want both myself and Miss Ella on the ground when you do that. For now, let's just take the car and go check out that road."

Bad Memories and New Lovers

As Larise drove away, she sensed Bran watching her. "What're you looking at?"

"The prettiest woman I've ever seen," he grinned. "I like looking at you. Is that so bad?"

"Yes. Well, no, but you're making me nervous and embarrassing me at the same time."

"What, you don't like compliments?"

"No, not usually, but I confess, I do like it, I'm just not used to hearing stuff like that from somebody who really means it, that's all."

"You're serious. You've never had anyone tell you you're pretty before?"

"Only when they wanted something from me or when I went undercover on the streets. I heard lots of men say I'm hot when I dressed up like a hooker."

"Yeah, that's not really a look I favor. I prefer the girl next door look, like now; boots, jeans, pretty top, light make up, ponytail, and ball cap. My idea of pure delight and super sexy."

That made her laugh. "Branimir the werewolf, you're weird and a perv. You think this is sexy."

"Yeah, you're getting me all steamed up. I'll be howling and pissing on the corners in a minute if you don't damp it down a bit."

Her laughter was full and rich and he grinned with delight. "You're a complete nut, you know that?"

"Da, I've been told that before, many times."

"What was her name, Elaine? The girl at the castle who teased you when you were in wolf form? Is she your girl?"

"Elaine is a dear friend, and she is playful with us, not fearful. She is quite beautiful, true, but she does not stir me as you do."

"Dammit, Bran, there you go again, spoiling the mood."

"Larise, why do you do that? Who has hurt you so badly that when I say I'm attracted to you, you pull away, put up your defenses?"

Larise didn't speak for a few moments, and he didn't disturb her thoughts. "I was engaged to a man who I thought loved me. We went as far as to hire a wedding planner."

"And then?"

"And then I came home early to find him in bed with my bridesmaid. In my bed that I shared with him. When I made an issue of it, he broke my jaw then sold the house while I was still in the hospital. They're married now, so I believe."

"You were betrayed. You loved, trusted completely, gave your heart, and he betrayed you. Thank you, Larise. Now I understand."

"None of that was true."

"I know. You're a terrible liar. So, who was it really?"

"Jimmy Vincent, fourth grade, I loaned him my crayons and the bastard broke them and my heart." Bran roared with laughter at that.

"This looks like it, Bran. 225 St. Elmo St.?"

"That's the right address. Let's see if anybody's home. Oh, don't show a badge unless you really have to. People tend to clam up when talking to a cop."

"Really? Now why have I never noticed that?"

"Shut up, Larise," he chuckled. She was grinning when he knocked on the door.

It took Bran a while, but he eventually got the old woman talking. Once she got going she broke down and sobbed her heart out on his shoulder. She'd been the only survivor in her family, and after all those years she was still haunted by the nightmares.

Composing herself at last, she went to the kitchen and made tea for them. When she came back she answered all his questions without hesitation.

Once they were back in the car Larise sighed. "Bran, I have no idea how you do that, but I'm jealous as hell. I'd sell my soul if I could get people to open up the way you do."

"It's no big secret."

"No, well then tell me, you big tease."

"I like them, Larise, the people. Each one has a special story of their own, and I understand that. I like them and they can sense that. I listen when they talk, listen to the story, the story of a life, experiences I will never have. Once folks realize you'll listen to their story and not judge them, they open right up. Sometimes that's the greatest gift you can give someone, to listen to their story and not judge them."

"Wow, now I'm in awe. You're for real with this, aren't you?"

"Yes, I am. I really like people and they sense this, they want to talk to me, tell their story. There, that's the next house, the blue one."

"So, how do you know this? I mean, as a werewolf you can't have spent a lot of time out in the general public, and you're still too young to have graduated from college."

"When we were brought out of the death camp I spent a lot of time with Clyde and Amanda. They taught me this."

"You spoke of this death camp before. Can I ask what that was?"

"There was a man, a criminal master mind. He learned of our existence in the mountains of Russia. He attacked us, killing most of the adults and capturing many of the young. We were then moved to training camps as he called them. We called them the death camps. We were forced to remain in wolf form, his savage dogs he called us.

He moved us from camp to camp while we were being trained to kill on command, and to do it as savagely as possible. "Those who fought back or didn't perform to his standards were killed. There were over fifty of us in the beginning. Barely twenty survived to come out. Without Igor's leadership we'd be lucky if there were five.

"Afterward we spent a lot of time with Amanda and Clyde, the Great Mother as well."

"Wow, Bran, it's amazing you're as functional as you are. What ever happened to that man, who was he?"

"His name was Stephan Krebs, Mr. Terry and Miss Gudrun killed him."

"So it was Gudrun Arielsdottir who brought down Krebs."

"Yes, they tracked him all over the world and finally finished him. I remember a great feeling of relief when I heard of it. There was always that fear of him in the back of my mind."

"Somehow I can't picture you being afraid of anything."

"Fear can be healthy by keeping you aware of danger. I fear many things, but I don't let it rule my life or stop me from taking risks, I just let it keep me aware of what the risk entails."

"Oh yeah? What's the biggest risk you've taken recently?"

She was grinning, but that vanished at his answer. "Falling for you. You don't trust me, and I can't seem to break past your natural fear of closeness. I could get hurt badly here, but I'll keep trying anyway."

Larise drove in silence for a while, and he didn't disturb her. As they neared the motel she spoke again. "Bran, I'm glad you don't give up easy. I want to, but not right now, not until this mission is over and that thing is dead, gone from my mind forever." He just gave her a gentle smile and nodded.

As Darkness Falls

It was a short drive to the turn off, then another fifteen minutes of rough road up into the trees to the place where the acolytes had camped. To the surprise of Igor's crew, they were there, and so was the sheriff. He held up his hand to stop them as they pulled over and got out.

"You people can't be here," he said, as he strode up to them. "Get back in that car and turn around. This is a crime scene, and you can't be here."

To the man's great surprise, the young blonde got right in his face. "Are you Sheriff Tanner?"

"What? Of course I am, the badge should have told you that."

"Okay," she replied, whipping out her own badge, "I'll see yours and raise you one." His eyes opened wide, and he backed up a step. "This man is Agent Wolf, he's in charge of this investigation."

"Since when did this become a federal case?" demanded the sheriff.

"Since one of our agents was sent back to New York in a straight jacket," said Igor, as he came around the car to stand beside Ronni. "Now, give me everything you've got on the latest murder here."

"I'm not giving you a damn thing. I don't know you people."

"You don't need to know us. Now give me what you've got on this, or face arrest for obstruction."

"I'd like to see you try to enforce that," he said, as he took a step back and reached for his gun.

42

To his utter shock the slim blonde took a swift step toward him, snatched the gun from his hand, and stepped back with it leveled at him. She had a hard look in her eye, and he swallowed the sudden lump in his throat.

"Don't ever try that again," she said. "Now step back and call whoever you want, but if you don't start cooperating, and soon, there will be repercussions." She popped the magazine from the gun, ejected the shell from the firing chamber, then tossed the empty weapon back to him.

"Just who the hell are you people?"

"You already know that," said Igor. "When one of our agents was returned to us in a straight jacket, the director put us on the case."

"So, what makes you so sure you'll do any better than the last one did?"

"Agent Parker was here to gather information, nothing more. She was attacked and abused by assailant or assailants unknown, injected with an unknown substance, then returned to us in restraints. That makes the director unhappy, so he called us in.

"Our team specializes in dealing with the unknown and unnatural. You've had something dangerous on your doorstep for years but did nothing about it. We're here to discover what that is, and to make it go away. This woman's death is connected to the mystery here and so, we'll be handling the investigation. Return to your office and prepare your files, one of our agents will arrive there to pick them up."

The sheriff glared at him for a long moment, then turned and stomped off to his car. As he drove past them, Ronni called out to him. He stopped and rolled down the car window. "What now?"

"You might want these," she said, as she tossed the parts to his gun through the open window and into his lap.

"Fucking bitch," she heard him mutter as he sped away.

Ronni turned to see Ella smiling at her. "What?"

"Enjoying the physical attributes of being immortal?" asked Ella.

"Well, he was being an asshole," she replied, blushing slightly. "Yeah, okay, I was. I got bullied a lot as a kid. It felt good to put one in his place for a change."

"He will cause us trouble," Igor said.

"Oops, my bad. Sorry."

"No, no, my pretty bird, you did right. You were gentler than I'd have been, and Miss Ella couldn't use the compulsion on him in front of so many witnesses. You did right."

"Yes, you did, Ronni," smiled Ella. "Igor's right, I couldn't use the compulsion in front of so many."

"Let's see if we can get anything useful out of these folks now," said Igor.

They didn't. All the people were sitting in a circle, chanting, and they refused to acknowledge the presence of the agents. Igor sighed and turned back toward the car. "Looks like we'll get nothing from these people at the moment. Perhaps we'll interview them one at a time later. Right now I want to get back and see what Bran has learned."

Darkness had fallen by the time they reached the motel once again. Branimir and Larise were waiting for them. "Learn anything new, Bran?" asked Igor.

"More of the same mostly," he replied. "A green mist, the man with the scar, the bull elk and several others."

"Others?"

"One woman said there were at least three elk changing into humans. I'm not sure about that one. She's quite old and a little fuzzy on some stuff."

"Larise, your impressions?"

"Oh, well, some of this is quite fantastic and, had I not experienced it, I wouldn't believe it," she replied. "However, we can say for sure there was a man with a scar on his face, the bull elk, and the green mist. What it all adds up to, I have no idea."

"Miss Ella, your impressions of what happened at the acolytes' camp?" asked Igor.

"I confess I paid little attention to the humans there, Igor. I let my senses roam a bit. Those people have all encountered the carue, but, for some reason it hasn't tried to compel them. However, it has somehow enlisted their assistance in protecting it's chosen lair."

"And the sheriff?"

"No, he doesn't carry the taint of the carue."

Igor nodded thoughtfully then turned to Kylie. "Kylie, your impressions?"

"Of?"

"All of it, especially the sheriff. There was something about that encounter that bothers me."

"Oh yeah," laughed Kylie. "He's hiding something all right. Actually, it was fun to watch Lady Hawk take that bully down a peg or two."

"Thank you, thank you, I'll be here all week," grinned Ronni.

Igor smiled with pride at his bride. "Your impressions, my love?"

"Yes, the sheriff is a bully, used to getting his own way by throwing his weight around. However, it really wasn't him who interested me, it was the others. They were all wearing an animal's claw around their neck, but keeping it hidden. There was also a nervousness about them, like prey sensing a predator."

"I agree," said Ella. "That's exactly what they reminded me of."

"Da, and me as well," agreed Igor.

"So, what's our next move, boss?" asked Kylie.

Igor grinned with delight when she addressed him as she always did Terry when on assignment. "First thing tomorrow, I want Larise to go up there to talk to those people. Larise, Kylie and Miss Ella will go with you for protection. Bran and I will scout the forest around their camp."

"And me?" asked Ronni, arching an eyebrow at him.

"You will be our eye in the sky, my pretty bird," said Igor. "Watch carefully and warn Miss Ella if the carue comes near.

"Now, I'm hungry. Larise, where can we get a decent meal around here?"

"There's a bar and grill just a block away. The food's great if you don't mind country music."

"I like country, and I'm hungry too," grinned Ronni. "Let's go."

The bar was typical of what one would expect. There were tables where folks sat drinking, some enjoying a meal. There was a pool table, in use, and a small space cleared for a dance floor. The music was loud and the conversations louder, Ronni grinned her delight as they stepped through the door.

They headed for a table just as the music paused. Ronni felt the hand grip her ass as the rough voice sounded right behind her. "Well hello there, little darlin.'"

Suddenly a big man leaped to his feet, dancing on his tip toes, Ronni gripping his fingers tightly and twisting them back and under. "You fond of those fingers, buddy?" she demanded.

"Yes, yes, please stop," he squeaked out.

"You planning to keep that hand in your pocket for the rest of the night?"

"Yes, yes, please..."

"All right then, you copped a feel. Was it worth it?"

"No ma'am, no, please ..."

"Sit down and keep your hands to yourself," she said, as she let him go.

The man sat down, nursing his injured hand. What happened next sent Larise into shock. Ella leaned over the man and spoke in a voice that dripped of old Southern charm. "Aw, sugar, that had to hurt. Come on, let's you and me go out back for a few minutes. Momma will take your mind off the pain, make it all better."

She took him by the arm and, looking somewhat dumbstruck, he rose and followed her out the door. As they left the bartender hurried after them. "Hey, we don't allow no hoo ..." Igor had stepped into his path.

"Don't say it, friend, don't even think it," he said, his voice low and dangerous. "When they return that man will have a smile on his face and all his money still in his wallet."

The bartender took a step back. "Oh yeah, then what the hell ..."

"The lady has needs. The rest is not your concern; go back to your bar."

Not knowing why, the man stepped back then returned to the bar. He was sweating. He couldn't say why, but that young man scared the lights out of him. He exuded danger, like a hungry predator.

Igor returned to the table to find the waitress taking the orders. "I ordered for you, sweetie," sang Ronni.

"Thank you, my love," he grinned, as he winked at the waitress. The aura of danger vanished and the girl favored him with a dazzling smile as she sped away to place the order. By the time she returned, Ella was leading her man back inside. She sat him back at his table and he refused to say a word to his friend, but he ordered a rare steak and a glass of red wine.

"Well?" asked Kylie.

"Not bad, but a little too much beer. I suggested he change to red wine, better for the blood." Igor chuckled at that, but Larise was just staring, open mouthed. Ella let her eyes change and her fangs extend slightly as she licked her lips. Larise swallowed hard and looked away.

"Down girl," chuckled Kylie, as she shook a finger at Ella and winked at Larise.

Just then a big man appeared at Ella shoulder. "My turn now, honey," he growled as he took her arm to drag her outside.

Ella pulled her arm from his grasp. "Not now, sugar. Maybe tomorrow, ask me then."

"I said now ..."

He got no further as Igor was between them, shoving him back. "The lady said no. No means no."

The man staggered back when Igor pushed him. "Why you dumb asshole, I'm gonna fuck you up ugly."

"I invite you to try," replied Igor, as he tossed his jacket to Ronni.

The man whipped out a knife, but the bartender stepped between then with a shotgun. "Take that outside, now. Igor nodded and turned toward the door as three more men rose from their tables to follow. Branimir started to rise, but Igor shook his head and Bran sat back down. The four men followed him outside.

Larise sat, wide-eyed, staring at the door. There were a few sounds of a struggle outside then Igor walked back in alone, rubbing his knuckles. He sat back down as the food arrived. "So, this looks good."

"Work up an appetite, did you, lover?" grinned Ronni.

"Da," he replied. "I'm hungry as a wolf." Kylie snickered and reached for the chicken wings.

They finished their meal and sat relaxing, listening to the music and just absorbing the atmosphere of a small town. Ronni was enjoying herself, especially when Igor danced with her. She taught him to do the two step. After a while they returned to the motel. As they walked along Igor could feel Larise's eyes on him. "What?"

"Are those men still alive?"

Igor grinned. "Of course. Bad manners isn't a killing offense, as far as I know. The challenge, that was a different matter. I defeated them, took their weapons, then left them there to revive on their own. As we left I could see that they had gone."

"So, you took what he said as a challenge?"

"Wasn't it?"

She sighed and put the key in the door. "Yeah, I guess it was." She started to push the door open, but Branimir put a hand on it to stop her. They all stepped away from the door and Ella slipped around to the back.

Larise covered her mouth with her hand as Igor shifted to wolf. He was even bigger and scarier than Bran. At the wolf's nod Bran flung the door open. Even as it swung open Igor leaped through. There was a scream inside then Igor called out. "Ronni, my pretty bird, would you bring my pants please?"

"What's it worth to ya?" she called back, her eyes dancing with mischief.

"Dammit, not now, woman, my captive is embarrassed, and before you say it, so am I."

Chuckling with delight Ronni gathered up his clothes and led the others in. A moment later Ella arrived with a man in tow. "Igor, put some pants on," she chided.

"Yes, ma'am," he sighed, rolling his eyes skyward. He stepped into his jeans and pulled a t-shirt over his head, settling it on his body.

"Just what the hell are you?" asked his female captive.

"Something very different from you," he replied. "The real question here is, what the hell were you doing in our room?"

"I'm the cleaning woman," she replied with a sneer.

Igor sighed and pushed her towards Ella. "Great Mother, could you encourage this woman to be a bit more forthcoming."

"Go ahead, torture me, I'll tell you nothing. I ..." The woman stopped speaking as Ella's eyes changed and her fangs slowly appeared. *"Be silent and stand still."* The woman was trembling in fear, her mouth working, but no sound coming out. *"You will answer all questions we put to you truthfully. Do you understand?"*

"I understand."

"She's all yours, Igor."

Igor approached to look the woman in the eye. "What were you doing in this room?"

"Searching," she replied, her voice flat and emotionless.

"What were you looking for?"

"Anything useful."

"Useful for what?"

"I don't know."

Larise saw his hand slowly curl into a fist and she shuddered. With a laugh, Kylie stepped in. "Igor, let me." He nodded so Kylie stepped up. "*You will answer this woman truthfully.*"

"I understand."

"Thank you, sweetheart," said Kylie, as she kissed Ella's cheek. "Now then," she said, as she turned to the woman who stood woodenly, waiting, "who sent you to search this room?"

"Sheriff Tanner."

"Did he tell you what to look for?"

"Yes. Anything that could be used as evidence of a murder."

"Did he say who we were supposed to have murdered?"

"Yes."

"Tell me who the victim was."

"The woman who was found near the hippie camp on the road to Whitbourne."

Kylie thought for a moment. "Are you a deputy?"

"No."

"Why do the sheriff's bidding?"

"He's my dealer."

"Well, isn't that just dandy," said Ronni.

"Hush now, sweet Ronni," said Igor. "Woman, did you know the victim?"

"Yes."

"Was she a user too?"

"Yes."

"Was the sheriff her dealer?" asked Igor.

"Yes."

"It becomes clear to me now," sighed Igor. "Miss Ella, can you send these people on their way?"

Ella nodded and pulled the man over beside the woman. *"You both searched our rooms. You found nothing of interest. You barely escaped as we returned. You were not seen. Go now and report this to the sheriff."* Without a word they both left the room as though in a trance.

Ronni sighed deeply. "Well, now we know what the sheriff's hiding. Man, I don't trust that guy. I'm going up for a look, make sure he isn't skulking around anywhere. You guys check to see if those two planted any evidence." With that she leaped at the open window and flew away.

It was many hours later the hawk returned, flying easily through the open window into the darkened room. In three easy strides she reached the bed and slipped beneath the covers. "Well hello there, sweet cakes," said a male voice that wasn't Igor's.

Ronni shrieked and leaped from the bed, flicking on the light. It was the man from the bar who'd grabbed her ass. "Well, well, it's you," he grinned as he drank in the sight of the gloriously naked woman before him. "See, I knew you'd come for a bit of old Jack's ..." He got no further as her fist cracked against his jaw and he was instantly asleep once again.

Swearing like a sailor, she leaped through the window and began to circle the motel. Two doors down she found the right window. Igor was still up, working at the computer. He looked up as she entered. "Ronni, what is it?" he asked as he saw the dark look on her face.

"I don't want to talk about it. Just shut off the damn light and come to bed."

"Sweet Ronni, what has happened to upset you so?" he asked, as he shut off the light, shed his clothes and took her in his arms.

"I said I don't want to talk about it. It's too damned embarrassing."

"Ronni?"

"No, you'll just laugh at me."

"My beloved Lady Hawk, Igor would never laugh at you. Come to me now. Tell Igor what wrong."

She sighed and melted back into his arms. "I was distracted a bit, and flew through the wrong window."

"Oh?"

"The room was dark. There was a man there who wasn't you, it was the guy from the bar. Hey, was that a snicker?"

"No," he denied, but another chuckle escaped him.

"It is, you're laughing at me. You beast, you're laughing at me. I got in bed with another man, and you think it's funny." She leaped astride his chest and began to beat him with a pillow.

Igor howled with laughter as he tried and failed to defend himself. "You miserable rotten beast." In spite of herself Ronni was laughing too. "Dammit, Igor, stop laughing at me and kiss me like you mean it."

"With extreme pleasure, my pretty bird."

Called

While Igor made Ronni forget all about her embarrassment, Branimir had another problem. Larise was talking in her sleep, but she wasn't speaking English. He shifted into wolf mode and approached the window, testing the air with his nose. Something was out there, something unnatural. At his low growl, she awakened.

Bran changed back and turned to her. "Arega ... who? Who are you? How did you get into my room? What ...?" Slowly she forced herself awake. "Bran? Bran, is that you? Oh dear gods, that was some nightmare."

Bran laid his finger against his lips for silence. He listened for a moment then spoke. "Larise, are you fully awake?"

"What? Yes, I'm awake."

"Go to the Great Mother. Go now, go quickly."

Before she could voice a question or objection he morphed back into the wolf and leaped through the window. Without thinking, she swiftly pulled on clothes and went to the room next to hers, knocking softly on the door. It opened instantly as Ella let her in. "Larise, what is it?" asked Kylie, as she rose gracefully to take the shaking woman in her arms.

"I don't know. I had a doozy of a nightmare. When I woke up Bran was at the window. He told me to come to you, then went all super wolf and jumped out the window."

"Something must be out there," said Ella. "Kylie, rouse Igor. Defend Larise until I return." With that she shimmered into the great cat and leaped through the open window.

Larise had watched her go. She turned to see Kylie with a gun in each hand. "Larise, come over here, take one of these and put your back to the wall. I need one hand free so I can call Igor." Larise did as Kylie asked and Kylie quickly called Igor's cell.

"Igor."

"It's Kylie. I've got Larise with me, Bran and Ella are on the hunt."

"We'll be right there."

A moment later there was a soft knock on the door. "Kylie, do you need help?"

"We've got this, Igor," she replied through the closed door.

"Ronni's already in the sky. I'll join the hunt."

"Understood." They heard him move away. "So, not really a nightmare?"

"Apparently not," sighed Larise. "It was ugly, truly ugly, I tried to fight my way out of it, but only made it halfway. I saw someone in the room with me, but didn't know who it was. It took a few minutes before I recognized him. I'll give him credit, Bran didn't move a muscle or speak until I was more awake. He told me to come to you then went wolf and jumped out the window. He was sniffing the air, listening, like he sensed something out there.

They had a while to wait, but eventually the hunters returned. The first was Ella, her naked form leaping easily through the open window to land in a forward roll that ended with her standing at the bedside, sweeping a robe about her shoulders. "Ella?"

"I caught a scent, but the wolves are on the trail. I'm more of an ambush hunter, those guys will follow a scent for days. Ronni's with them, scouting from above. How she can see anything from that height at night is anybody's guess, but she can."

At that moment the hawk swept into the room and morphed into Rhonda. "The boys are on their way back. Whatever it was it ran straight to the camp on the road to Whitbourne. Those self-titled peace-loving pagans were all packing shotguns, so Igor and Bran turned back."

Just then the wolves came leaping through the window, shimmering into Branimir and Igor. "Jesus, don't any of you people believe in clothes?"

"Aw, Larise, are you sure you don't like it?"

"Shut up, Bran," she said, turning slightly away and blushing furiously. "Just shut the hell up and put some pants on."

Ronni laughed and stepped toward the window. "Hang on guys, I'll bring you some clothes." She flew through the window and disappeared. A few minutes later there was a soft knock at the door. Kylie answered it and Ronni, wearing a long flowing dress, entered carrying jeans and t-shirts for both men.

They swiftly dressed then Igor spoke. "Okay, we're all wearing pants now, can we move on to what the hell happened? Bran?"

"I awoke to sounds, both in the room and outside. Larise was talking in her sleep, she seemed to be fighting something. There was a rustling outside and a faint scent of something, fox and not fox, foul smelling, like blood and mold.

"I shook the bed lightly and she started to wake up. I waited until she was fully awake, then I sent her to Miss Ella before I went after whatever was outside. There was no time to call you, I could sense it moving away."

Igor nodded. "Miss Ella?"

"I sensed someone approaching our door. I was awake and reaching for it even as Larise knocked. I asked Kylie to alert you then I joined Bran on the hunt. I, too, caught that scent, fox and more, or perhaps less, but not fully fox. I continued to follow, but when you ran past me

I turned back, knowing I can't keep up with you wolves, and that we'd left Kylie and Larise unguarded."

"You did right," smiled Igor, "and I thank you for it. Ronni?"

"We got the call and as you changed into the wolf, I went up for a look. I soon found Bran on the trail with Ella and you closing in, so I went on ahead. I caught sight of the running fox just as it reached the camp and disappeared inside a tent. I started my circle to the left then saw the shotguns so I dropped down to warn you."

"Thank you for that, my pretty bird. We'll return to that camp in the daylight. Kylie and Larise in human form and the rest of us as wolf, hawk, and tigress. We will investigate the surrounding area while you ladies keep the camper's attention elsewhere.

"Now, Larise, what can you tell us?"

She sighed and plopped down on the edge of the bed. "It was a nightmare. I was being pulled back to that town, drawn there. I lied to you earlier, Igor, I can sense that thing, in a way. It's like it's calling to me, pulling at me to return.

"In the dream I was doing just that. It was there, half elk, half man, and raving wildly. It grew fangs and reached for me, that's when I started to fight my way out of the dream. Something broke the spell, probably Bran shaking the bed. Thanks for that, buddy. The rest you know."

"Why did you lie to us about that?"

"I don't really know, it just sort of slipped out, and then I was reluctant to change what I'd said. This shit is starting to scare me, like I'm not entirely sure who's in control here, me or that thing, and the closer we get to it, the longer I'm here, the worse it seems to get."

"Miss Ella?"

"Of course, Igor. *Larise, look at me. Relax, you are aware of the creature that calls to you. That calling is a thin line we can follow to find this creature, extract vengeance for what was done to you. That calling is just a distant voice, it has no power over you at all. You are in full control of your faculties at all times. There's a thick fence that protects you from that voice in your mind. You are safe behind that fence, Larise.*

"There now, that should do it."

Larise visibly relaxed. "Wow, that's pure magic, you know that?"

"Can you sense anything near now?" asked Igor.

She shook her head as did the others. "Me either. I think it's safe now for us all to get a bit more sleep. Good night, family." With that they returned to their separate rooms and went back to sleep, all except Branimir. He sat watching her sleep and wondering. His wolf had already chosen her for a mate, but he wondered, could she do it? Trust? Could he in turn, trust her?

"Are you certain you'll be all right?" Ella asked Kylie the next morning before they all set out.

"I'm fine," she replied. "You guys go see what you can discover. Larise and I'll keep the natives distracted." She stepped into Ella's arms and kissed her cheek. "I'll watch her, my love, I won't turn my back."

She did though. They stopped the car and got out before they reached the encampment. The shapeshifters changed then slipped into the trees. Rhonda took two steps then leaped skyward. She was soon circling lazily to the right high above.

"Some days I feel like my momma," chuckled Kylie, as she gathered up and folded the discarded clothing the shapeshifters had left behind.

"I get that," grinned Larise.

They got back in the car and approached the camp.

The two wolves and the gigantic tigress prowled the forest around the camp, staying out of sight, but barely. Finally, they turned their attentions further up the mountainside toward the abandoned town. They could easily smell the intruder from the previous night, and there were others. They followed that scent until they reached the cleared area where the ghost town lay.

The scent of their prey was mixed with many more, all bearing the mark of a single dominant, but the town was empty. After a fruitless search they turned back, not willing to leave Kylie alone with Larise for too long. They were right to worry.

Back at the campsite things were starting to deteriorate. One large man stepped forward. "Look, we've answered enough of your questions. That one (pointing at Larise) isn't allowed here anyway. Now, we've cooperated, but we're done. You need to leave. Now."

Kylie felt the atmosphere shifting. The docile campers were suddenly getting aggressive. The team needed more time. She got right in the man's face. "You see this badge? Well this badge says you answer as many questions as I decide to ask. If you have a problem with it, we can haul your sorry ass into the jail, give you a few days to think about it, then ask again."

She felt him tensing. Stepping back, she whipped out her gun. "Larise, cover me." She got no answer. "Larise?"

Larise was struggling. She'd pulled her gun at the same time as Kylie, but something caused her mind to go foggy. She didn't seem to recognize the woman calling her name, nor could she understand what the woman wanted. Slowly her arm came up to aim the gun at the woman speaking the strange language. "Arma dre ..." She got no further as the hawk screamed a challenge and dropped from the sky.

Sharp talons raked at Larise's arm and strong wings beat at her face. The gun was sent flying. Larise managed to bat the bird aside, but to her horror, it morphed into a naked woman and rolled to its feet. Two swift strides and it was a hawk again, rising swiftly into the sky. Before anything else could happen, something screamed in terror.

As all eyes turned as an animal raced from the trees and through the camp, two huge wolves gaining on it. As the campers went for their rifles, there came the battle roar of a saber-toothed tiger. Guns were dropped from nerveless hands as the massive cat was suddenly among them. It charged through the camp, striking Larise with a shoulder and sending her flying. Two gunshots followed.

Larise came back to herself as she picked herself up from where the tigress had knocked her down. She heard the two shots and saw Kylie holding one gun on the campers and one on her.

"That's far enough," said Kylie, and the campers froze in place. "Larise, get your ass behind that wheel or I'll drop you where you stand."

Larise believed her. She nodded and got into the car, started the engine and waited until Kylie got in with her. She was acutely aware of the gun Kylie kept trained on her. "Kylie, what the hell's going on?"

"You tell me."

"I don't understand."

"Neither do I. I thought we could trust you, but if Ronni hadn't spotted you taking aim at my head I'd be dead right now. You even fart wrong and you go back in a body bag this time. I do not fuck around with this shit."

"I believe you, but I don't understand. I pulled a gun on you?"

"You did."

"I don't remember doing that. Christ, my head hurts, and my arm. Why is my arm bleeding?"

"Your arm hurts because you pulled a gun on me. The Lady Hawk dropped down and ripped it away from you. Could be why your head hurts too."

"What do you mean?"

"She smacked you upside the head a few times with her bony wings. You'll probably get a shiner from it." Kylie sighed and put her gun away. "Can't remember any of it?"

"Just that damned tiger knocking me ass over breakfast. Jesus, my head ..."

"Stop there, by that clearing. We'll pick up the rest of the team." Larise pulled over and they got out of the car.

Kylie came around the car to her just as the tigress burst from the trees. It morphed into an angry vampire as it reached them. Ella's hand clamped over Larise's throat, lifting her off the ground even as she reached for Kylie. "Kylie, are you hurt, are you ...?"

She reached for Ella's arm and pressed down gently. "Let her go, love. I'm fine, and she doesn't remember much of it. Let her go now."

Ella set Larise back on her feet then thrust her back against the car with a snarl. "Easy lover, easy" said Kylie. "Once the boys and Ronni get here we need to figure out what the hell's going on with this thing." Even as Kylie spoke, Rhonda alit and transformed. She swiftly pulled on her clothes then reached for the first aid kit.

"Show me the arm, Larise." Hesitantly, she extended the arm, but the woman who bandaged her was as gentle as the hawk had been fierce. Igor and Branimir soon arrived and shimmered back to human form.

"Is it dead?" asked Ella, as they pulled on their clothes.

"Da," replied Igor, "it's dead. It was a fox, or it once was before it was changed. Larise, can you understand me? Is your head clear?"

"Yes," she replied, with a nod of thanks to Rhonda.

"So, what happened? Kylie?"

"We stalled as long as we could, but suddenly they began to get nervous, and then aggressive. I pulled a gun to stop them then Ronni dropped out of the sky and saved my ass. I owe you one, sweet sister." Ronni just winked at her.

"Larise?"

"Igor, I don't know what the hell happened. At first it went according to plan. Kylie asked a lot of questions, they tried to evade, we learned nothing new, but then it started to get fuzzy. I heard angry voices, words I couldn't understand. Someone was calling my name, but I couldn't understand her. She scared me and I pulled out my gun. I didn't want to, but couldn't stop myself, and then the hawk attacked me. Ronni, thanks for that.

"I fought her off, then you guys chased something through the camp, the tiger knocked me flying, and I came to with Kylie pointing a gun at my head."

"Great Mother, why does the compulsion not hold on Larise? Is she like Kylie?"

"Sadly no, Igor. Larise isn't immune to the compulsion. She's been marked. That's the only thing stronger than the compulsion."

"Marked?"

"Like Gina marked Marco, as Gudrun marked Terry."

"Ah, I see."

"I don't understand," said Larise.

"A vampire can mark a human in a way that creates a permanent emotional and telepathic link," said Kylie. "Ella marked me when we bonded for life. In an emergency the vampire can mark someone to use them as needed."

"No, no, I ..."

"Larise, recall when you fought the elk/man. Did you bleed?"

"Yes."

"Did it bleed?"

"Yes, I had a knife and cut it."

"Did you get its blood on your face, your lips?"

"Yes, I believe so."

"Did it taste your blood?"

"Yes, it bit me, but I escaped."

"So, there you have it people," sighed Ella, as she relaxed her posture. "Larise, forgive me, I should have thought of that possibility in the beginning. I apologize if I hurt you."

"Hurt me? You scared the crap out of me, both as the tiger and as the vampire. Sweet Jesus. So, you're telling me this thing can take me over, control me, and there's nothing you can do about it. Is that right?"

"There is one thing, and one thing only, we can do to release you from its grip," replied Ella. "We have to kill it."

"Until you do, I'm a clear danger to you. I know you have to kill me." Her eyes misted over and her hands trembled. "Please, just make it quick."

"Whoa there," said Branimir, as he gently took her in his arms. "Nobody's killing anybody right now. Igor?"

"Relax, Bran, I won't shoot your girl, but you've got to keep a reign on her."

"Understood. It'll be my pleasure to keep her close."

"What??? His girl? Keep me close? What the hell are you guys ...?"

"Easy, girl, easy," grinned Ronni. "Look, we don't have to kill you, but we do have to keep you under observation until we can break you loose from the monster."

"So I'm back in the straight jacket?"

"No, you're already in the trap."

"What?"

"I will keep you close to me, Larise," Bran said, as he held her gently. "We'll hang out at the motel, go back to talk to the deputy, drive Kylie nuts, stuff like that."

"Oh yeah, so what happens if it takes me over again?"

"I won't let you leave; I won't let you hurt anyone. I'll always be right at your side until this is over and you're free of it all."

"Thanks, I guess."

"Oh come on, you might like it."

"That's what I'm afraid of."

"Come on, let's go back to the motel," said Igor. "It's getting late and I'm hungry as a bear."

"What? Weren't there any mice in the woods?" Ronni asked, a merry twinkle in her eye.

"Woman, it's cruel to tease the starving," sighed Igor. She just giggled and snuggled into his arms.

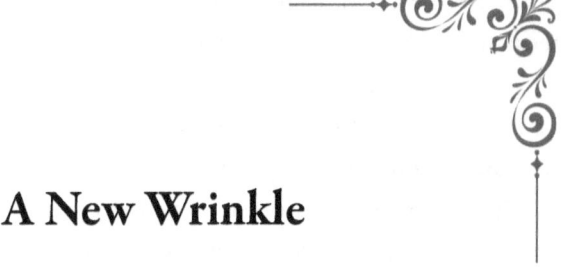

A New Wrinkle

B ack in the motel after a meal, they sat together, mulling over the day' events. Igor noticed Ella gazing into the distance. Suddenly she was on her feet heading for the door. "Stay here, I'll be right back." She stepped through the door and into the night. It was much later when she reappeared.

As Ella returned to the room it was clear she was unhappy. One look at her eyes silenced all questions. She sat brooding for a few minutes before she spoke. "I should have known; it was the only possible answer."

"Great Mother?"

"There's another vampire involved here, Igor. I can sense it, now that I'm aware of its presence. I was too focused on the carue to catch the awareness of the other."

"Another vampire? Could Mobutu truly have returned from ..."

"No, Igor, not Mobutu, but one of his creation. I can sense it clearly now, for it's close, curious about us, but extremely wary none the less. There may even be more. From what you've learned from the people who lived in that town, there was a mass killing frenzy, a full reign of terror. A single carue couldn't have managed it, and according to accounts, Mobutu merely watched, enjoying the spectacle.

"I believe he made several of them, both vampire and carue. He has done this before several times, created vampires, turned them loose, then when he got bored with them, killed them himself, for he believed himself to be a god. I suspect this one, and the carue, escaped him and returned to this familiar area when he left.

"There's probably an affinity between the vampire and the carue."

Igor nodded thoughtfully. "Okay, so we have a vampire to locate for you. Where do we begin, here in this town or ...?

"No, Igor, in the forest. I wandered the town this night, and, although I sensed it near, I got no sense of a lair, of possessiveness, as in a hunting ground to defend. No, forgive me, but I believe this one is a child, living in the forest, surviving off animal blood as well as unsuspecting hunters and hikers. That's why the bodies are never found, it kills then drags the bodies away to a hidden lair for reasons of its own.

"All this is just supposition, of course, but it's my best guess."

"I won't bet against you," said Igor, reaching for his ringing phone. "Igor here."

"Igor, it's Sally. Igor, I've had a terrible premonition. Tell Ella it's another vampire."

"Yes, Queen Sally, the Great Mother has already discovered this."

"Igor, the beast is a child, and yet not a child. Be extremely careful."

"Igor, this is Harald. Do you need reinforcements, another vampire perhaps?"

"Thank you, Sire, but I believe we can handle the situation."

"Igor, don't let pride blind you. Ask for help if you need it."

"I will, my king, trust me. Igor will be careful."

"All right, Igor. Remember, help is available if you need it."

"I will, Sire. Thank you."

"Very well then, Agent Wolf, carry on." With that the king broke the connection.

Rhonda stepped behind Igor and rested her hand on his shoulder. "Honey ..."

"I know, my pretty bird, the game has changed. We're no longer searching for information, we already know most of what we need to know. There's just one more wild card I'd like to pin down."

"And that is?"

"The sheriff. Miss Ella, if you had never met Terry before, could you tell if he'd been marked by a vampire?"

"Yes, if I was watching for it, or if I was alone with him for a few moments, why? Do you suspect the sheriff?"

"Da, I do. I saw his car go by a few moments ago. He's still hanging around and I don't like it. I'd like to send Kylie and Larise back to the Lair so Bran can help me hunt the carue and vampire for you. With Ronni in the air and two wolves on the ground we should have no trouble finding them."

"Actually, I think we need to keep Larise with us," said Ella. "Her presence will help hold the carue in the area, perhaps even the vampire. Kylie should return though."

"Oh no you don't, Ella West," declared Kylie. "You're not putting me on a shelf to keep me out of the action. I can handle myself and I can keep an eye out for Larise if Igor needs Bran for the hunt."

"Kylie, my stubborn girl, will you not let me keep you safe?" sighed Ella.

"I'll be careful, and I'll stay back out of the action, but I'm part of this team, I'm staying."

Ella looked to Igor, who shrugged his shoulders. "So, the team stays together, then we hunt as a pack, together. First thing tomorrow I want to have a talk with that sheriff where Miss Ella can watch him closely. This man is a problem, and we need to know just how big that problem is."

"So, what if he's just a nosy old cop?" asked Larise.

"Then Miss Ella can put the compulsion on him, and no harm done," replied Igor. "On the other hand, if he's a servant of the vampire then we will have to deal with him, keep him out of the action until the vampire is dead. For now, we get some rest."

While the others slept, Ella hunted. She could sense the other vampire now and tried to zero in on it. All to no avail. It was aware of her as well, and was avoiding any contact. At one point Ella caught a glimpse of something darting through the forest but was unable to run it down. It had looked like a child, but she knew better. This creature was a killer. Finally, Ella sensed the other one moving further away and she returned to the motel.

Deep in the forest, a small creature huddled beneath a rock overhang. Cuddling the remains of an old rag doll close to her chest, the forever young vampire talked to the doll, her only friend and companion throughout her long lonely life. "It was her, Maggie. It wasn't Momma, and it wasn't the bad man who hurt us. It was a grown-up woman, but we can't eat her Maggie. She's too dangerous.

"I know you're hungry, So am I. Carue is hiding from the bad woman too, maybe his camp of humans isn't guarded. Yes, I know, Carue will be angry, but he's hiding now and even if he knows he can never catch us. We can eat one of his humans and watch when he goes all crazy, won't that be fun, Maggie. Come on, the bad woman has gone away now."

As silent as a sigh of wind, she slipped away and approached the camp of the people on the road to Whitbourne. There was only one animal on guard, and she laughed at its screams as she leaped on it and tore it apart. The campers clutched their guns tight as they listened to those screams.

The silence of a forest night fell, then lingered, and nothing happened. Eventually a man emerged cautiously from a tent, then slunk off towards the latrines. He didn't make it. A child-sized creature, dressed in ragged ill-fitting clothes, blocked his path. He watched in horror as it snarled and flexed its clawed hands.

The man screamed in terror and dropped his rifle as it leaped at him. He continued screaming for help as it tore at him, finally fastening needle sharp fangs into his thigh. He beat at it feebly with his hands then slowly fell to the ground, watching through horrified eyes as the vampire slaked her burning thirst with his life's blood.

No one answered his call for help. Slowly he faded into darkness, and she continued to feed until there was no more blood to be had. Sated at last, she retrieved her doll and fled into the forest, away from the town and the dangerous woman there, dragging the body behind her. Away from the carue, too.

"Now we feel better, Maggie. I know you do too. Maybe that sheriff will bring us something good tomorrow. I'll call him to us; he knows better than to come without presents."

NEXT MORNING THEY LOCATED the sheriff back at the acolytes' campsite. They'd heard screams in the night and now a man was missing. For some reason the sheriff seemed uneasy with Igor and his team there. "Agent Wolf, what are you doing here?"

"Wondering what you're doing interfering with my case."

"What do you mean, your case? I'm here to investigate a murder."

"Are you? Where's your victim?"

"Well, he's missing. These people heard screams in the night and today there's a man missing."

"I see. Still my case."

The tall woman had been watching the sheriff closely. When Igor turned to her she nodded. Igor turned back to the sheriff. "Sheriff, I'll ask you to hand over your firearm now. You're under arrest for interfering in a federal case."

"Now wait just a minute here. There's no fucking way in hell I'm ..." He got no further as Igor moved. The sheriff was instantly down on the ground, disarmed, and in restraints.

"Agent Hawk?"

"Yes Agent Wolf?" Rhonda's eyes were twinkling with mischief.

"Would you be so kind as to search the sheriff's car for me?"

"It would be my pleasure, Special Agent Wolf." It didn't take her long to find a hidden container of drugs as well as three vials of blood.

"Well, would you look at that," grinned Igor, as he hauled the sheriff to his feet. "Sheriff, you're under arrest for impeding a federal investigation, possession of a controlled substance for the purpose of trafficking, and suspicion of murder."

"Now listen here ..."

"No, you listen, you have the right to remain silent, and I do suggest you exercise that right. Bran, you and Larise take the sheriff to jail and make sure the deputy books him properly, take his badge and pin it on that deputy. Tell him to keep this man behind bars."

Nodding, Branimir took the sheriff by the arm and settled him in the back of his own cruiser. Larise drove while Bran sat quietly in the passenger's seat, ignoring the ruckus from the back. Kylie followed in one of the SUVs.

The prisoner threatened, begged, prayed, and fought, kicking at the barricade between them. He had to get free, she was calling to him. He had to break free and go to her. It took Bran and the deputy both to get him out of the car and into a jail cell.

"Agent Parker, just what the hell happened here?" asked the deputy, as Branimir pinned the sheriff's badge on him.

"The former sheriff ran afoul of what happened to me, just not quite as bad. It was just dumb luck we discovered the drugs hidden in the cruiser."

"Let me out," shouted the prisoner. "I have to go to her. Let me out of this fucking cell or I'll kill the lot of you."

"You might want to add uttering threats to that list of offenses," grinned Larise, as she and Bran left the office.

"Are you okay, Larise?" asked Bran, as they got back in the car with Kylie,

who'd followed them to the sheriff's office.

"Sure, I'm fine. Whatever got its hooks into that guy, I can't feel a thing. Now, how about explaining Igor's remark."

"Igor's remark?"

"Don't worry, Bran, I won't shoot your girl? Your girl? Care to tell me what that's about, Mr. Super Bodyguard?"

"No," replied Bran, looking away and blushing.

"No?"

"No."

"Kylie?"

"The boy's got a case for you, girl. Couldn't you tell?"

"Yeah, I know, but ... Listen, Bran," sighed Larise, "my head is still all messed up, and that damn thing could take control of me at any moment. There's no telling what I might do when ..."

"Nothing," he replied gently. "If that happens I'll hold you until it passes and you'll do nothing to hurt anyone or yourself."

"You'll hold me?"

"It's my job," he grinned.

"And you don't enjoy it at all."

"Larise, is it so bad if I enjoy my work?"

She sighed deeply and leaned against him. "Listen you, I need to get this monkey off my back and sort myself out before I even think about anything else. Do you understand?"

"Da, I understand, but it's still my task and my pleasure to protect you, even from yourself. I'll always be right beside you until this is finished."

"And then?"

"And then it will be up to you to choose."

She sighed again and snuggled closer to him. "Thanks for that."

While Branimir and company delivered their prisoner to the lock up, Igor was having a bit of fun with the people back at the camp.

"So, Mr. Government Agent, just what the hell is she?" demanded one woman as she pointed an accusing finger at Rhonda.

Igor quirked an eyebrow at the woman. "She's the medical officer on our team."

"That's not what I mean, and you damn well know it."

"Excuse me?"

"I saw her. She changed into a bird; I saw it. The bird attacked that other agent then it changed into her and then back into a bird and flew away."

Igor grinned. "Really? Changed into a bird?"

"Damn right she did, and don't you try to deny it."

"I suppose there was a saber-toothed tiger and three dinosaurs running through the camp as well."

The woman was angry now. "Yes there was, well, the tiger anyway, and those two giant wolves."

"A tiger and two giant wolves?"

"That's right. So what do you have to say now, Mr. Government Agent?"

"I say you folks have been using some of the sheriff's wacky candy."

"What the hell does that have to do with anything?"

"You were hallucinating with the drugs. Dr. Stockman will now check you over to make sure you're all right."

"What? No friggin' way, I'm not hallucinating, and she's not touching me. I saw what I saw."

"A woman who turned into a bird, a saber-toothed tiger, and two giant wolves? Is that your story?"

Slowly the woman began to back away from him. "No, no. I didn't see anything, nothing at all." She turned and fled behind the others.

Igor winked at Ella then spoke loud enough for all of them to hear. "Listen up, people. I'll give you the rest of the day to get yourself together. When I come back tomorrow, you'd all better be gone. Anyone I find tomorrow will be hauled away and charged with obstruction and drug trafficking."

"Hey, you can't run us off like a bunch of kids. This is America, we've got religious freedom. We can stay here and worship our god all we like."

"This is public land," replied Igor, "not a designated church. You will leave or we will remove you." With that he turned away and they left, returning to the motel.

When they reached the motel, Ella went to get some rest, Igor reported to the king, and Rhonda took to the sky. She wanted to keep an eye on the campers.

Lying on a gentle updraft, the hawk made a wide lazy circle to the right. She saw them easily, even though, to them, she was just a speck in the sky. They were packing up their camp. It looked as though Igor's threat had the desired effect. Continuing her circle, she watched, then suddenly became more alert. The campers weren't leaving, they were headed for the ghost town.

The campers made their way toward the sacred ground but stopped at a tight turn in the road. From high above the hawk watched as they set up a barricade, then settled down behind it. She turned back toward the town, but soon spotted a saber-toothed tigress prowling the former campsite. She dropped down lower and gave a piercing cry.

The big cat instantly raised her head, searching for the source of that cry. The hawk was making a tight circle to the right. As the cat moved in her direction the hawk flew away. The tigress followed and soon saw the hawk making a tight circle to the left up ahead. Suddenly the hawk changed directions and made a tight circle to the right.

The tigress stopped and watched as the hawk returned to her. The bird dropped to the ground, morphing into Rhonda as she touched down. The cat shimmered back into the vampire. "Ronni, what is it?"

"Ella, the campers have set up a roadblock. They're armed and worse, there's a number of wrong animals joining them."

"Wrong animals?"

"Animals that have been changed, like that fox the boys chased through the camp. I think we'll have a tough time getting past them where they're set up."

"Very well then," sighed Ella. "Let's return to the motel and see what Igor has to say about this development."

"Race ya," laughed Rhonda as she leaped into the air, morphing into the hawk again.

Smiling and shaking her head, Ella West morphed back into the tigress and set out for the motel. Since appointing Harald as king, Ella found herself with something she'd yearned for all her unnaturally long life, friends and family, people who knew what she was and loved her anyway. In spite of everything they faced, life for Ella was good.

Igor listened as Rhonda and Ella filled him in. A snarl crossed his face as he mulled it over. "Talk to me, tall, dark, and furry," said Rhonda, as she snuggled close to him.

With a rueful smile he put his arm around her. "I feel like I'm losing all control of this situation," he sighed. "Perhaps the king should have sent Terry anyway."

"Hey, since when does my big bad wolf give up? Come on now, put that thinking cap on and get busy. We need to get a grip on this thing. Come on, sweetheart, work through it. We got the sheriff out of the way, what's our next move?"

"Well, I could call the king and ask for Eric to bring the rest of the wolves here and take Kylie and Larise back to the lair where they'll be safe. Then the pack hunts and eliminates the problem of the animals, Miss Ella destroys the carue. With all that mess out of the way she can then hunt the vampire with the help of the wolves."

"But? What else is bothering you, honey?"

"Two things. First the green mist those people spoke about. You're the scientist in the family, my pretty bird. Any ideas."

"Actually, I do," replied Rhonda. "There are a lot of hot springs around these parts. Hot springs are heated by volcanic activity. I think one of those meteors from Ella's time struck this area, hit a soft spot, and went deep. I think it melted down and perhaps was thrown back out into the air with a bunch of other volcanic gases.

"It may have helped to change some of the animals, but I doubt it. I expect it merely enhanced the terror of the townsfolk that day."

"A weird coincidence?"

"That's my theory, lover."

Igor sighed and mulled that over for a moment. "So, Sweet Ronni, the green shit isn't a concern?"

"I don't believe it is."

"Okay, so, now I face the last obstacle."

"And that is?"

"Alpha's pride," sighed Igor, as he cuddled her closer.

"You don't want to call the king and ask for help?" asked Ella.

"No, I was given my choice of people who could help me get this done. Now I feel like I'm failing all of you too."

"Actually, that's not quite how it happened, Igor," smiled Ella. "The king told you to pick your six-agent team, Terry's fault for limiting your options. I then insisted on bringing Larise with us instead of keeping her safe at the lair. That further limited your options. You then had to assign a protector for her, another limit.

"Igor, you've failed no one here. If you don't want to ask for more help then it's up to the three of us, you, me, and Ronni."

"Da, I'll stop whining now," he sighed. "It's time for us to do this thing. Sweet Ronni, how many animals did you see helping the humans?"

"A dozen, no more, but the humans have shotguns. Igor ..."

"Hush now, my pretty bird, let Igor think." Rhonda fell silent and no one broke his mood. A few moments later he gave a rueful grin. "Da, so be it. Sweet Ronni, give me your solemn oath now that you will not try to get into the fight. I need you to stay safe."

"Igor ..."

"Promise me now, my pretty bird."

"All right, but only if you swear you'll hold nothing back."

"Ronni?"

"I know what you're capable of, my lover. There's nothing on Earth except Ella herself that could stand against you if you give it your all. So, promise me you won't hold back, not for any animal, nor for the humans. Swear it and I'll stay out of the action."

"Yes, my pretty bird, Igor will hold nothing back in a battle with these things, human or animal."

"So, tomorrow we hunt together?" asked Ella. The grin on her face made Larise shiver.

"Da, Great Mother, tomorrow the wolf and tiger hunt together. We will transform then bypass the humans who blockade the road. We will approach the town by another path. With luck we'll find the carue and you can make an end of him. That will release Larise from his power then Bran can help us locate the other vampire."

"We have a plan," said Ella. "Now we should head for the bar where we can all get a good meal. I want us both well fed for the hunt." Once again Larise shivered at the look in the eye of the vampire.

As they entered the bar, Ronni started moving to the music. She grabbed Igor and dragged him onto the dance floor. With a grin of mischief, Branimir took Larise by the hand and spun her onto the floor too. Startled, she almost protested, but he was moving her through the dance before she had a chance.

Kylie commandeered a table while Ella scanned the room. Spotting her quarry, she moved towards him. As his companions fell silent, the man looked up from his beer to see the gloriously beautiful woman approaching. "Your turn, let's go," she said, as she patted his shoulder and headed for the back door.

With a sloppy leer on his face, he stood and followed her outside. His world went all to hell as he stepped through the door and reached for her. She grabbed him by the throat and hurled him against a wall, driving the air from his lungs.

He tried to speak, but his voice froze in his throat as he saw her face. Her eyes had changed to cat's eyes and long fangs protruded from her upper jaw. Before he could get his voice back she was on him, a powerful hand forcing his head up and back while needle sharp fangs bit deep into his neck. He tried to struggle, but it was futile.

Ella fought herself to keep from drinking him dry. She thrust him back, licked the blood from her lips then returned her appearance to normal. He tried to crawl away from her, but she grabbed him by the scruff and hauled him to his feet.

"*Stand still and be silent. You will never speak of this experience as long as you live. You will count to twenty slowly then return to your place in the bar. You have had the best sex of your life, but you will speak of it to no one. You will never approach me again. Begin.*"

It's All Gone To Hell

E lla returned to find Kylie sitting alone at a table, the others still
dancing. "Did you have a good meal, my darling?"

"I did, Kylie. Have you ordered for the others?"

"I did, yes. It'll be here in a moment." She was right, the food soon
arrived and with it, the dancers. They enjoyed the food, the music and
dancing, but Ella was being watchful, more than usual. Her senses were
on full alert, something wasn't right here, but she couldn't quite put a
name to it.

Eventually they returned to the motel and retired, but Ella slept
lightly. Finally, deep in the night, she arose and went to Igor's door. She
could hear them asleep inside, so she moved on to Larise's room, but
she heard nothing from inside.

A hard twist of the wrist and the lock broke. Inside Ella found an
open window, a pile of Branimir's clothes on the floor with blood on
them, and no people. In an instant she shimmered into the tigress and
leaped through the window. The scent of Branimir's rage mixed with
his blood was easy to follow.

Kylie had awakened as Ella rose from the bed. Her head out the
door, she saw as Ella entered Larise's room. She followed in time to see
the tigress vanish through the window. She hurried back and knocked
on Igor's door.

"What is it, Kylie?" asked Rhonda as she opened the door.

"Something's happened. Larise and Bran are gone, there's blood in
their room, and Ella is on the trail."

"Shit," exclaimed Rhonda, then she leaped skyward through the window with a piercing cry.

"Shit," muttered Igor, as he ran to Bran's room. A quick look around and he morphed into the wolf and leaped through the window.

"Sure," muttered Kylie, "leave the human to pick up after you, bunch of shapeshifters." She began gathering up the discarded night clothes.

BRANIMIR STOPPED RUNNING, his sides heaving, and shook the cobwebs out of his eyes. His head ached abysmally where she'd struck him. She had a good head start on him, but he was gaining ground, if only he could keep going. Still in wolf form, he rested until his vision cleared then ran on. As he ran he heard the cry of the hawk high overhead.

The terrain steepened and he tired swiftly. Again he stopped to catch his breath. Before he could continue the hawk swooped down beside him and morphed into Rhonda. "Transform, Bran." He obeyed the alpha female of his pack. "Where are you hurt?"

"My head ..."

"Kneel down now so I can get a look at it."

"It's okay, I'll be fine ..."

"Do like Dr. Ronni says, Bran," she said kindly. "Let me get a look at that." With a sigh the tall youth sank to the ground at her feet. "Wow, she clocked you a good one, buddy. I'm going to have to sew that up."

"There's no time, Ronni, I have to get her back ..."

"It's too late for that, big boy, she's already reached the barricade and joined the acolytes. Way too many guns for us to go charging in. We need to go back so I can patch you up and you can report to Igor."

Her heart broke as he seemed to melt to the ground. "I failed him," he sighed. "I've lost the girl and failed the pack. I'll be lucky if he doesn't drive me out."

"He'll do no such thing; I won't allow it. You didn't fail, Bran, you were blindsided. Can you tell me what happened?"

"Da, I heard something outside the window. She said she was scared, and I put her behind me as I slid the window open. Next thing I knew I woke up, soaked in my own blood, my head aching like fire, and Larise gone."

"You stay here, Bran. I don't want you moving around until I sew up that gash on your head. Promise me you'll stay put until I get back."

He nodded, but she gave him a piercing gaze and he chuckled. "I promise, Lady Hawk, I will wait for your return." She patted his shoulder and leaped into the sky.

Ella was slowing down. "I'm an ambush hunter," she grumbled to herself, "not a goddamned cheetah." Just then the dire wolf blasted past her. With a snarl she picked up her pace. A moment later she heard the cry of the hawk ahead. She soon found Ronni and Igor in a small clearing. Ronni told them where to find Branimir then flew off.

They found the wounded wolf easily and he brought them up to speed. Shortly they heard the cry of the hawk as the bird came in carrying a small first aid kit in her talons. She morphed into the woman and began patching up the injury on Bran's scalp. "Hold still and it won't hurt so much. There now, that should do it. Swallow this, it'll help cut through the pain and clear your head."

Bran swallowed the pill then turned to Igor. "I failed you, Igor. Do you want me to leave the pack?"

"No, old friend, you must stay with the pack, I need you. Also, it is I who has failed you here. We knew this woman couldn't be trusted, and worse, I knew she's a trained agent. I should've known she would find a way. I should've known she would try to hurt you to escape. I should ..."

"Stop talking now," said Rhonda. "Look, we're all here, Larise will be safe enough with those people for now, if we all skirt past them and kill the carue, that'll set her free forever. It'll also set the rest of them free, so they'll be no threat, right? No big problem to get her back once we've killed the monkey on her back. So, let's quit yakking and get to work."

"Ronni?"

"She hurt one of our people, Igor. It's not her fault, but we know whose fault it is. It's time for us to show what happens when one of our people gets attacked." Without waiting for an answer, she leaped into the sky.

"Where is she going?" asked Branimir.

"She's hunting the carue," replied Igor. "Come on, with any luck we can keep her in sight." They set out after her, but hadn't gone far when they heard the rifle shot and saw the hawk fall from the sky. The falling bird changed into a naked woman as it fell.

With a heart rending howl Igor leaped ahead. Branimir and Ella found him in human form, cradling the broken body of his lover. Before they could reach him the second shot rang out and blood spurted from his shoulder.

Igor shifted into the wolf and the next shot missed him. He vanished into the thick brush as Larise crept out into the open. Her instincts were sharp, the wolf attack missed, and before he could recover and kill her, the weapon was stripped from her hand and she was held in Branimir's arms. The tigress leaped to Bran's defense and that was all that saved his life.

Still in wolf form, Igor faced the huge tigress, a snarl on his face. Moving easily from side to side he watched for even a hint of an opening. The battle that would cause his death was forestalled by a soft groan behind him. In an instant he turned, transformed, and had Rhonda in his arms, tears of relief streaming down his face.

"Gods, I hurt," groaned Rhonda, as she struggled to sit up. "Anybody got anything to eat, I'm starving."

"You wait here with Miss Ella, my pretty bird. Igor will bring you food."

"Igor, don't ..." It was too late; he'd already transformed and vanished into the trees.

Rhonda struggled to her feet then approached the others. Branimir stepped into her path, but swallowed hard at the look in her eye. "Step aside, Bran, step aside or die where you stand."

"Lady Hawk, I ..."

Ella transformed and stepped in front of Bran. She took Rhonda in her arms and hugged her gently. "Easy, my sister, easy. Wait until Igor returns with food for you. I know how you feel, what you want to do, for I have been there many times. Control it, fight the hunger and the rage. Wait for Igor before you do anything."

Rhonda returned the hug then stepped back. "All right, but I need a favor from you."

"Anything, little sister, what do you need?"

Rhonda pointed at Larise, who was trying to break Branimir's grip and escape. "Drink that one into weakness so she can't cause any more trouble."

Ella nodded, then with a speed that staggered the mind she spun around, seized Larise with an iron grip and sank sharp fangs into the woman's neck. Larise screamed and fought, but it was useless, she was held fast in the vampire's grasp. Branimir reach toward Ella, but he was seized from behind and hurled away.

The cold icy look in Rhonda's eyes broke him and he sat down, gazing at Larise, tears streaming down his face. As the helpless woman went limp in the arms of the vampire he lowered his head into his hands and gave one long mournful howl as he tried to release her from his heart. He'd have given his life for her, but that was not to be allowed. His position in the pack would be reduced, and it would be a long time before he'd able to consider a mate again.

Ella thrust Larise away and she slowly sank to the ground and tried to weakly crawl away. Rhonda grabbed her by the leg and dragged her back. That's when they heard the gunfire. Several shotgun blasts were followed by screams of terror and pain, then all was silent.

A few moments later Igor came limping back into their small clearing, carrying a backpack. He went straight to Rhonda and took her into his arms, kissing her face, gently running his hands over her body, making certain she was actually in one piece. "I'm all right, my beloved. I'm fine, my big bad wolf. Did you bring me any food? I'm starving."

Igor reached into the backpack and began to hand her food, meats, cheese, protein bars, bottles of water. Rhonda devoured them all and looked for more. "That's all I could find in their camp, my pretty bird. I'll go back and see if I can find more."

"No, stay with me. I'll be fine for a while, I will, I promise. Now, let me look at your wounds."

"I'm fine."

"You're not, but I think you'll keep until I can get you back to the hotel."

"We'll go soon, but first we have to find the carue and make an end of it."

A soft groan from the ground caught their attention. Larise was holding her head and moaning. "Jesus my head hurts. I feel sick, so weak. What's happened to me?"

"So, you're yourself again, are you?" said Branimir, as he grabbed her by the hair and hauled her to her feet.

"Ow, let go of me, you asshole. What the hell's wrong with you, Bran?"

"I'll tell you," he snarled, as he pushed her back against a tree. "You hit me from behind, split my head open. By the time we caught up with you, you had a rifle, and you shot the Lady Hawk. I saw her fall from the sky to be broken on the ground. I heard the howl of agony from my pack leader as he watched his beloved fall.

"Igor reached her broken dead body and held her, that's when you shot him. You're a traitor, you've killed one of ours who was trying to help you, you shot our leader and tried to kill him, and you've destroyed me. Thanks to you I must now face Igor in battle or run away and hide in the forest until he finds me to finish me.

"I loved you, woman. I risked everything for you, and you betrayed my trust, my love. You're feeling weak because the vampire has drunk most of your blood to keep you alive. Had she not done so the Lady Hawk would have killed you, she may yet."

Larise pressed herself back against the tree, her eyes wide with horror. She knew he spoke the truth, this young werewolf didn't have it in him to lie. She reached toward him, but he pulled away. "Bran?"

"No, do not dare to touch me." His shoulders slumping, he turned away. Tears ran down her face as he returned to Igor and transformed. The big wolf sank to the ground and rolled on its back, exposing its throat and belly.

Branimir nearly went into shock as Igor knelt and rubbed his belly. "Get up, you damn fool. I didn't risk my life a dozen times keeping you alive in the death camp just to end you over a woman. Get up."

Bran morphed back into the young man and stood up. "Igor, I challenged you. You can't let that pass, you can't."

"So, who died and made you king? I'm the alpha, I can do whatever I want. Bran, you did what I told you to do. I told you to protect her at all cost, and that's what you did, even going so far as to get in my face to do it. Next time I give you an order I'll be more careful how I word it."

"But, Igor ..."

"Be easy, old friend. There is our beloved Lady Hawk, whole and sound, and as fierce as ever. We're all right here."

"Not yet, you're not," said Rhonda, as she stepped up beside him. "I need to get you back to the motel so I can deal with that shoulder wound, and, may the gods forgive me, I need to get a decent meal into me."

"You're still hungry?" asked Igor, raising an eyebrow at her.

"Yes, she is, Igor," grinned Ella, "and she will be for a while yet. Ronni, take to the air and go back, fill Kylie in on our adventures, send her with the car and some clothes to pick us up, then head for the bar and get some food into you. We'll join you as soon as we can."

Rhonda looked to Igor who kissed her cheek and nodded. She leaped into the sky and vanished into the morning sun, the mountains echoing her piercing call.

Ella turned to Igor. "I assume that barricade is no longer being manned."

"Those who survived ran away. They may have returned by now, but I doubt it. Bran, you are no longer bodyguard to this woman, I'll watch her myself." He fastened his gaze on Larise and she swallowed hard. She saw only a swift death in those eyes. "Come." With downcast eyes she came.

Igor gazed at her for a long moment then spoke. "Larise, I don't blame you for what happened, I blame the carue. However, there are questions, questions that need answers. For example, how did the beast know for you to shoot the hawk?"

"It would have read that from her mind, Igor," said Ella. "It would have recognized the hawk was a threat. I believe also that this is why the carue keeps trying to reacquire Larise. It instinctively understands the value of her skills and abilities. Igor, this is all my fault. Had I realized at the beginning that she'd been marked, I'd never have asked for her to be brought along. Forgive me."

"There is nothing to forgive, Great Mother," sighed Igor. "You didn't know, nor did we. This is the nature of the job, yeah? You learn as you go and deal with whatever is in front of you."

They began walking towards the roadway, Larise staying meekly by Igor's side. "Miss Ella, how far can the carue reach her?" asked Igor. "If she was far away could ...?"

"It wouldn't matter, Igor. No matter where she is, that abomination can reach her, and now, understanding her value as a servant, it'll work ceaselessly to retrieve her. Look at her. Her eyes are glazing over, even now it calls to her."

Igor's fist snapped out and cracked against the woman's jaw. She sank to the ground, unconscious. Igor reached down, tossed her across his shoulder, then continued on toward the road. They reached the road and started downhill, but soon heard the car coming.

"Suit up, folks," said Kylie, as she pulled over and stopped the car. "We have to get back before Ronni eats the cafe out of food."

"Take Bran and Miss Ella to the cafe, company for my sweet Ronni," said Igor. "I'll stay with Larise and report to the king. You can bring me some food, if there's any left."

"Igor, what are you going to do?" asked Ella.

"I'll swallow my pride and ask the king for help," he sighed. "It's that or kill Larise, and I don't want to do that."

"Thanks for that," came a soft voice from the floor beside him.

"This isn't your fault, and you shouldn't pay the price for it," he replied, his voice still hard, "but I can't trust you, even Bran couldn't trust you for an instant."

"What are you going to do with me?"

"I'll send you back to the lair. They'll keep you confined until this is over, then we'll see from there. Once out from under the influence of the carue, you may yet prove useful, trustworthy. For now I'll see you kept safe, but confined so you can't hurt anybody. I'll ask for another agent to replace you on the team."

"You should just kill me, Igor. That's the only way to be sure."

"Shut the hell up or I might."

They reached the motel and Igor dragged Larise into his room and shut the door. She sat quietly on the bed while he reported to the king. His eyes never left her and she knew, this was a very different wolf.

"That's wise, Igor," said the king. "Who should I send to you?"

"If possible, Sire, send Miss Gudrun to take her back to the Lair. This woman is dangerous and can't be trusted as long as the carue lives. Put her in a cell and be very careful when feeding her. Once this is all over perhaps Mr. Clyde and Miss Amanda can help her, but not now."

"I understand. Who do you want on your team?"

"I would prefer a vampire if possible, Sire. We not only have the carue to deal with, but there is another vampire as well."

"A vampire it is, Igor. We'll have someone there before nightfall today."

"Thank you, King Harald. I'll ask Kylie to drive down to that same airport with me and pick them up."

LARISE'S EYES GLAZED over and she began to struggle as the car sped away from the town and back toward the small airport. Those efforts to free herself went unrewarded as Igor slid his arms around her neck and applied pressure. The woman fought for a moment then relaxed in his grip.

"Sleeper hold?" asked Kylie, as she drove on.

"Da," replied Igor. "Eric taught me that one. He said it would be handy and he was right."

"So, what are you going to do about Bran?"

"Do?"

"He's hurting, Igor. He believes he let you down, worse, he challenged you, and he can't understand why you didn't drive him out or kill him."

"He didn't challenge me, Kylie. He did as I asked him. I'll make him understand the fault here is mine. As soon as we realized she'd been marked I should have sent her back. I didn't fully understand the power of the mark, but held back so he could remain near her, hoping his feelings for her could break the spell. I misjudged that, and my friend pays the price for my mistake."

"You have to talk to him."

"I know, but first I get rid of the problem, then I talk to Bran, make him listen."

"You also have to find a way to restore his confidence, help him understand you still trust him, look to him as your second in command."

"Now you sound like Eric or Miss Gudrun."

Kylie laughed at that. "Come on, Igor, you know I'm right."

"I know, Kylie, I know. I'll talk to him as soon as we get back."

She nodded as she turned in towards the air strip where they found the plane. They saw Gudrun with her crew waiting for them. Larise was groggy but awake as Igor hauled her from the car. He shoved her toward the plane and Jimmy caught her to steady her. "Ow, what the hell?"

Jimmy grinned as he supported her weight. "Go to sleep, little girl, go to sleep."

"You dirty bastard, you drugged me."

"Yes, my ducky, I did indeed. We were told you could be dangerous. Besides, Eric is a terrible pilot. You'll have a more enjoyable flight if you sleep through it."

"You prick, I'll ..." Her voice faded as she melted into his arms. Grinning, Jimmy picked her up and carried her onto the plane.

"Vassily, you and Jimmy watch her carefully," said Igor. "You can't trust her, not until we've killed the thing that controls her. Be wary, she's tricky and treacherous."

"We will, Igor. Relax, Jimmy's got her out cold, she's in restraints, and we'll both watch her closely until we have her in a cell at the Lair."

"Even then, Vassily, even then."

"Yes, even then, until you give the all-clear." He squeezed Igor's shoulder then followed Jimmy back onto the plane.

Igor turned to Gudrun and raised an eyebrow at her. "Hi, I'm Gudrun, your new recruit."

That made him laugh, bringing the first smile to his face since he'd seen Rhonda fall. "Miss Gudrun, I'm glad you're here, I desperately need your advice." Igor proceeded to fill her in while Kylie drove them back to the motel.

THEY ARRIVED TO FIND Ella waiting for them. Igor went on full alert at the first glance at her face. "Great Mother, what has happened?"

"Far too much, Igor," sighed Ella. "The sheriff escaped custody, shot two people, and dragged another away with him. He was last seen headed this way."

"And?"

"Bran disappeared. We think he's gone after the carue. Ronni went after him before I could stop her." She was startled at how fast he transformed and raced away.

Ella was still sputtering when she noticed the grin on Gudrun's face. "What?"

"The young can be so impetuous, can't they?"

"Shut up, Gudrun," sighed Ella. "Now what the hell are we supposed to do?"

"From what I understand," said Gudrun, "there's a road leading to the carue's hideout. Now we hitch a ride with Kylie and follow them. We're the back-up team."

"Quickly then," said Ella, as she leaped aboard the car.

"You don't think the boys can handle this carue?" asked Gudrun, as the car sped up the dirt road toward the town of Whitbourne.

"Perhaps they could kill it if that's all they faced," replied Ella.

"All right, so what else is there facing them?"

"Other controlled animals, humans with guns, and possibly another vampire."

"Not good odds. Do we have weapons?"

"There's a couple of side arms in the trunk," said Kylie, "but that's all."

"Shit. That's not helpful," sighed Gudrun. "What the hell's that?"

"The barricade," replied Ella. "Igor left a few of them alive. I'm actually surprised they returned here."

"I've really got to talk to that boy about leaving live enemies behind," grumbled Gudrun. "Just give me a minute."

She hopped out of the car and approached the barricade. "Turn around," shouted a large woman. "turn around and git." She got no further as Gudrun suddenly moved. There were screams of pain and bodies flying everywhere as the warrior vampire struck. In mere moments all five humans were dead. Not one had managed to get off a shot.

Gudrun threw the bodies into the trees then pushed the barricade aside. She walked a few paces up the road, carefully looked all around, tested the air for scent of more enemies, then turned to face the car and stuck up her thumb.

"Jesus, woman," said Kylie, as Gudrun climbed back into the car. "Did you have to kill them?"

"Yes." Gudrun endured the silence for a moment then relented. "They were armed, controlled by the enemy, Kylie. They had to be neutralized. We have agents behind enemy lines, facing enemies both known and unknown. As well, we have no intel about enemy numbers. No way in hell I'm leaving a live enemy behind me when I go in blind."

"She's right, Kylie, my love," sighed Ella. "Gudrun's the best there is, we'll defer to her until we rejoin with Igor."

"Yeah, you're right," agreed Kylie. "If that thing could turn Larise against Bran, those people would surely have come after us. Sorry, Gudrun, you did right."

"Relax, little sister, I've just had way more practice at this than you have. Okay, is that the ghost town up ahead?"

"Yes. Pull over and let us out, Kylie. You turn around and go back to the hotel in case somebody returns."

"Yes ma'am. Got your cell with you, Gudrun?"

"I do, but don't call us, we'll call you."

"Oh sure. I've heard that one before."

"Stop it," chuckled Gudrun. "We have to be serious now." She shimmered into killing vampire mode as Ella shifted to the tigress. Together and fully alert they entered the town. A moment later they heard the sounds of battle.

The Hunt Goes On

They'd watched Igor take Larise away. Ella'd sighed and patted Branimir's shoulder as she turned back toward the motel. With a startled curse the hawk exploded into the air right before her. "Fuck!"

Ella leaped back then spun around to see the wolf disappear into the trees with the hawk in pursuit. She'd started to transform, then changed her mind, there was no point. "Dammit, no way in hell I could catch those two. Bring him back, Ronni, bring him back alive."

With a fierce determination the dire wolf had attacked the mountain side, keeping to the thick brush so the hawk couldn't head him off. "I failed you once, Igor, I won't fail you again." Settling in to a hard pace, he continued to climb toward the abandoned town.

It was a long hard run, but he finally neared his target. He rounded a huge boulder to find Rhonda waiting for him, her fists on her hips and a fierce look in her eye. "Well, have you managed to burn off some of that energy, or do you want to do a few more laps?"

Tongue hanging from the side of his mouth and his sides heaving as he gulped in great lungsful of the crisp mountain air, the wolf faced the woman. Finally he lowered his head and transformed. Rhonda sat and patted the ground beside her. Meekly, he came and sat. "Well?"

"Lady Hawk, I failed at my task, I lost my place in the pack, I failed my alpha, I lost the woman I loved."

"So, what was your plan?"

"Find the carue, kill it, regain my place in the pack, then mourn the loss of her. That or get killed, then it wouldn't matter anymore anyway."

"Oh, for pity sake. Men." Rhonda sighed and put her arm around his shoulders. "First, you didn't fail, we did. Second, your place in the pack is the same as it's always been, Igor's second. You're a natural leader, Bran. Igor needs, and wants, you right where you are in the pack. Third, sorry buddy, but that carue will likely kick your butt."

"I don't care."

"Yeah, well I do, so give that up."

"What am I to do, Ronni?" His voice cracked as he spoke, and her heart broke for him.

"Find the carue. I'll help you, but, from there we make a plan. You watch him while I go for help." He nodded, but she tugged on his ear. "I mean it, Bran."

"I will obey, Lady Hawk. I promise."

Rhonda ruffled his hair and grinned. "If you've got your fingers crossed I'll smack you, buddy. Come on, let's go find an ugly beast." She rose then leaped into the air. He morphed back into the wolf and trotted into the empty town.

Bran took his time, searching everywhere for a trail to follow. It took a long time, but he eventually found a fresh scent. Nose to the ground, he trotted around a corner and right into a trap, only the hawk's warning cry saved him.

The two wolves attacked, but soon realized their mistake. The intruder was too big, too fast, and far too savage. With a maddened fury he tore into them, venting his rage at his failure and the woman's betrayal, on the two aggressors. In moments one was dead and the other trying to flee. It did no good, the dire wolf ran him down and finished him.

As Bran stood over the last fallen attacker the hawk alit and transformed. "Are you hurt?" For a reply the big wolf merely shook himself then trotted back to the corner, snuffled about until he had the scent again then set off. The hawk returned to the sky, watching carefully. Bran was soon alerted by her cry. He turned another corner to see a bull elk looking back at him.

They stared each other down for several moments then the wolf took a step backward. The elk bugled a challenge and reared up on its back legs. Slowly, bellowing all the while, it began to change. With a snarl of pure rage, the wolf attacked.

Caught halfway through the change, the carue fought back, but the wolf took a terrible toll. Eventually the monster managed a glancing blow that sent the wolf flying to land hard. Struggling to get air back in his lungs, Branimir nevertheless got back on his feet as the now fully transformed carue charged. Worse, it was healing.

As fast as the beast was, the wolf was equal to it. Ducking under a powerful blow, the dire wolf bit deeply into the beast's thigh. Again the wolf was battered away, but now the carue was seriously wounded. Snarling his hate, the wolf circled his prey, searching for an opening. Both combatants were injured, but the carue was healing, the wolf wasn't.

The wolf suddenly changed direction causing the carue to lurch as it turned to face him, it was the opening he needed. Before the carue could fully react, the wolf had him by the throat. Suddenly terrified, the beast tore the attacker off him and hurled it away. Branimir landed hard, but he'd seen what the carue had not. He leaped to his feet and charged.

The carue braced to meet the attack, but something hit it from behind, something bigger, stronger, and even more savage. As Igor knocked the beast off its feet Bran leaped in to grab it by the hamstring, ripping and tearing at it. Howling, the carue tried to batter him down, but Igor had it by the throat. Both wolves were tearing at the downed carue when the second carue arrived.

It bellowed and charged, but suddenly stopped and spun around. The battle roar of the saber-toothed tiger echoed through the mountains as the mighty beast hurled itself upon the second carue.

The carue turned to flee, but there was no hope. It fought with all its strength, but it was helpless in the jaws of the tigress. In mere moments it was dead, its head nearly severed from the body.

Ella transformed and turned to see Gudrun pass a small first aid kit to Rhonda, who then set about tending the two warriors who sat side by side near the carue they had managed to finish. "Damn thing was hard to kill," grumbled Igor.

"Yeah," agreed Branimir. "Thanks for the save."

"The save? You had it beaten when I got here, I just didn't want to be left out of the fun." Bran just grunted and grimaced as Rhonda dabbed something on one of his shoulder scratches. "Just like the old days, eh Bran? Remember how we used to double team that fat guy in the death camp. He used to crap himself even before we started."

Bran chuckled at that. "Da, he didn't know who'd attack him first. We make a good team."

"We do," agreed Igor. "So, no more bullshit about breaking up the team, leaving the pack?"

"Igor, are you certain about this?"

"Would I be here if I wasn't? Why are we still talking about this? Stop sulking and come home, we've got work to do."

Suddenly the carue at their feet twitched. Gudrun grabbed it by the antlers, and with a hard pass of her knife, severed the head and hurled it away. She did the same with the second one as Ella approached the werewolves. "Do you two characters know what you've done?"

Both men stood to face her contritely. "Great Mother?"

Ella stepped between them and hugged them. "You two actually brought down a carue. Until this day I could never have imagined it. Ronni, I have no idea how you survive living with such savages."

"Ah, they're not so tough," grinned Rhonda. "They whimper like puppies when I stitch them back up."

"Lady Hawk, please, leave the wolves some dignity," said Igor. She grinned and ruffled his hair then kissed his cheek. "So, you and Bran went hunting without me."

Rhonda sighed then spoke. "The plan was to find the carue, then I'd fly back to get you guys. Bran gave me his word he'd only watch until you arrived."

Igor turned to Branimir. "So, what happened?"

"I found the scent and started to follow. I turned that corner and got ambushed by wolves, wrong wolves. Only the Lady Hawk's warning saved my hide. I dispatched the wolves then started tracking the carue again, but it jumped me."

"Ah-huh."

"It did, Igor. Ronni, tell him."

"Yeah, it did. It must have heard or felt the wolves getting their asses kicked and came running to help."

"And it jumped him?"

"Well, they faced off like a couple of gunslingers for a while then Bran took a step back. That's when the carue attacked."

Igor grinned at Bran. "Works every time, doesn't it?" Branimir blushed and shuffled his feet. Igor looked at the two dead carue and shook his head. "How many more of these accursed things are there, do you think?"

"Who knows," said Rhonda. "But the fact that there were two of them is a bit disturbing."

"Yes, it is," agreed Ella. "And there's more. As we saw, they can return from the lands beyond. How do we make certain that doesn't happen?"

"I'll deal with that," said Gudrun. "First, I want to know why there were armed people at that barricade? Why were they still alive?"

"The barricade is new, Miss Gudrun. My first visit was after sweet Ronni revived. She was hungry so I went to the barricade for food. I killed a number of them, but didn't take the time to hunt them down. I returned to Ronni as quickly as I could."

Gudrun nodded and patted his shoulder. "You did right, Igor." She passed Ella her phone then tore the antlers from the two skulls. Ella called Kylie and as soon as the car arrived, Gudrun put the carue heads in a garbage bag. "We'll find a crematorium somewhere and make sure those things don't revive."

"That's a job for Gudrun and Kylie," said Rhonda. "I'll fly back and pick up the other car, bring you warriors some clothes." With that she leaped skyward and swiftly disappeared from sight.

"What is it, Miss Ella?" asked Igor.

"The other vampire is near, probably saw the battle. It's moving away now. We'll wait here for Ronni to return. We've had enough excitement for one day."

THE SMALL VAMPIRE SLUNK back to her safe cave, snuggling down with her doll to watch the body of the sheriff. Perhaps she'd beaten him too hard this time. "The bad woman is too strong, Maggie. She turns into a tiger too. She's way too dangerous for us to fight. They killed both carues too, his old one and my new one. We have to leave and find a new home."

She sniffed and hugged the doll tighter. "Don't worry, Maggie. I'll find us a better place, closer to where we can find food. Maybe we should take him with us. He's an adult so he can go places we can't. He can bring us food too. I know, Maggie, I know. He'd better not come without treats again or we'll eat him then find another adult to be our daddy."

EVEN AS LIFE LEFT THE carue at the jaws of the dire wolves, Larise awoke from the drugs with a soul searing wail of torment and loss. She lay on the floor of the plane sobbing uncontrollably. "What the hell?"

"Easy, Eric," said Vassily. "I think Igor just sent the all-clear. Let's get her up onto a seat, Jimmy, I think we should get some food into her." Together they lifted the distraught woman onto a seat. Jimmy held her gently while Vassily brought her food. She sat listlessly and ate what they gave her but showed no other interest in life at all.

Freedom

Larise sat quietly as the plane landed. She'd reluctantly eaten the food these men had given her, but her heart wasn't in it. As they stepped down from the plane she saw a group of armed men and women waiting for them, the weapons were pointed at her. She didn't care, she was already dead inside.

Suddenly the queen came hurrying up to them. "Stand down, people, stand down. This woman is no threat to us now."

The king was there as well. He turned to Sally, giving her a quizzical look. "My love, are you completely certain?"

"I am, Harald. Larise doesn't need armed guards now, she needs Amanda." She reached out and took Larise by the arm. "Come on, we'll take you to Clara, get you checked out, then we'll settle you into a room and send for Amanda."

Larise didn't respond but followed meekly along. She was completely empty inside, broken, cold, and empty. The queen led her to the same room she'd occupied when she'd first arrived at the castle. Elaine was already there with fresh clothes and a pot of hot tea. She bowed slightly to the queen, then fled the room.

Sally sat Larise by the window, then brought her tea. She got another for herself then sat facing the near comatose woman. Neither one spoke, they just sat quietly gazing out the window. At length, another woman arrived. She smiled at the queen who nodded then left.

"Hello, Larise, I'm Amanda. We didn't get a chance to meet when you were here before."

Slowly, Larise looked up at the woman. "So, you're the shrink?"

Amanda grinned. "What was it, did the queen warn you, or do I have a sign on my forehead?"

The tiniest smile touched the girl's lips. "It was the sign. So, you're supposed to put me back together now?"

"Are you truly broken, Larise?"

"I have no idea, but I probably am."

"Can't you tell?"

"I was broken, too many times before, now I'm just empty, nothing in there at all."

"Too many times before? When was the first time?"

"When I was thirteen, my uncle got drunk and you can guess the rest."

"Yes," sighed Amanda. "Sadly, Larise, you're not the first in that department. I'm sorry that happened to you. I assume he got away with it. Is that why you went into police work?"

"Yeah, that was a big piece of it all right. The thing is, I got put onto the vice squad, luring in johns looking for young hookers. I hated that job."

"Can't blame you there. Catching all those abusers didn't erase the first incident, did it?"

"No. I'd hoped it might, but ..."

"You said too many times."

"Yeah, well there was the macho attitude around the physical training which I loathed. That just made me bitter. Eventually I made it to special agent, but not before my partner double crossed me and damn near got me killed."

"So that, added to the earlier experience, gave you serious trust issues."

"Yeah, it sure did." Somehow this strange, sad looking woman had managed to reach in and flip the switch inside. Larise silently berated herself for it, but she couldn't seem to stop babbling out all her tightly held secrets."

"Larise, I've spoken with Ella just moments ago and she explained what happened to you."

"Apparently, I got marked by that thing, whatever it was."

"Yes. Ella believes the carue marked you, but you managed to escape it. It later realized your value and skills, so it tried to reacquire you."

"You mean it succeeded." She suddenly burst into tears and was instantly held in gentle arms. "Amanda, I remember pointing my gun at Kylie, I remember the love in Bran's eyes, I remember shooting the hawk and trying to kill Igor, too."

She paused and tried to sniff back her tears. "Oh god, I remember the hurt in Bran's eyes as he cursed me for a traitor." She shuddered then slowly regained control. Amanda released her and returned to her own chair.

"Can you describe what it felt like when the connection to the carue was severed?"

"That was like having my heart torn out for the second time. I hated that thing, hated that it could control me, that it could make me turn on those who depended on me, who trusted me. Still, it was a strange connection that brought a sense of peace and comfort when it activated me. Everything went away except the desire to make the beast pleased with me.

"When it died, it tore the heart from me, and yet I felt a great sense of relief, almost exultation at being free from its chains. That lasted for only seconds then I was empty inside, no thoughts, no desires, nothing at all except empty. It wasn't until the queen touched my hand that the memories started to come back."

Amanda smiled at that. "Yes, our Sally does have a special magic all of her own."

"Yes, well, I won't thank her for it; she did me no favors there. Are they going to kill me?"

"No, Larise, they aren't going to harm you."

"Is one of the vampires going to make me forget everything?"

"That I cannot say. Larise, let's go back a bit. Tell me what interested you before the original incident."

"Seriously?"

Amanda smiled at that. "Yes, seriously. What did that twelve-year-old girl dream of becoming?"

"Oh god, how the hell should I know? It's been so long since I could dream. Botany, I wanted to develop new medicinal plant species."

"Tell me, how did that catch your interest."

Larise blushed and gazed out the window. When she spoke, her voice was sadly wistful. "My dad and I watched an old Batman movie. One evil character was Poison Ivy. I remember Dad saying that with her abilities she could do so much to help mankind, new medicines, new food sources, stuff like that."

"And you pictured yourself as the good Ivy."

Larise gave a gentle smile. "Yeah, I did."

"Did you ever make any moves toward that dream?"

"No, I started helping Mom with the flower gardens, but ..."

"I understand," said Amanda, gently patting her hand.

"Amanda, I feel empty inside again. I remember it all now, and I know I should celebrate being free of that abomination, ..."

"But?"

"But I've got a huge hole inside me, an abyss that I'm afraid will swallow me whole. Do you think that will ever go away?"

"I'm sure it will in time. I'll talk to the other vampires, see if they have any experience or knowledge that might help us understand what's happening for you. Larise, give yourself time, time to rest, time to heal. I'll come back for a chat every day for the next while. For now, you get some rest and I'll station someone outside to make sure you're left in peace."

"You mean to make sure I don't make a run for it."

"No, Larise, she'll be there to protect your privacy, and to help you with anything you need."

There was a soft tap at the door. "Come in, Marta. Larise, this is Marta."

Larise looked at the smiling young woman and sighed. "You're a werewolf, aren't you?"

"How could you tell?" asked Marta, as Amanda slipped silently from the room.

"Your name sounds Russian, you have a Russian accent, and the werewolves are Russian, therefore, werewolf."

Marta laughed as she sat by the window. "Da, I'm werewolf, but I'm also woman, farm helper, secret agent like you. I was trained as assassin before these people helped us break free of the one who controlled us."

Larise gazed at this friendly young woman and relaxed. She sensed no threat at all. "Farm helper?"

Marta chuckled with delight. "Da, there are two farms attached to the castle. Farmer Bill runs them. When he first came he spoke of getting a dog to walk the fields with him in the morning, so Olla goes wolf every morning to walk with him. Lately she has had to help her mate with the children, so I go instead.

"Larise, I'm here to be both a protector and companion to you for a few days, unless you'd prefer another."

"No, it's okay. Amanda says they're not going to kill me, so I guess I should start building a new life. As prisons go, this place is pretty comfortable, and the jailers seem friendly."

Marta nodded and patted her shoulder. "Get some rest, Larise. I'll be right outside." With that she rose and walked out, closing the door behind her. Larise just sat staring out the window, trying to will away the memories of the past weeks and doing her best to ignore the gaping hole in her soul left by the death of the carue.

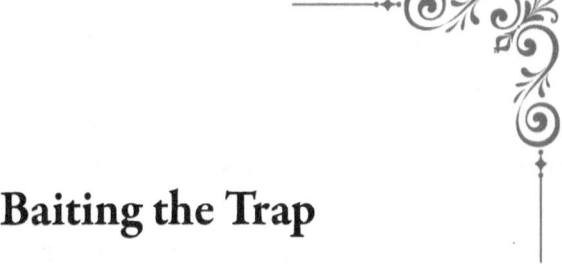

Baiting the Trap

Both Ella and Gudrun kept their senses on full alert, but the vampire had moved away. Soon Rhonda arrived with the car and some clothing. They returned to the motel, then Gudrun and Kylie left in search of a crematorium. It was much later they returned. "Job's done, boss," grinned Kylie as they got back. "So, is anybody hungry?"

"Da," groaned Igor, as he levered himself to his feet. "Let's go to the bar and eat. We can confer and make a new plan once we've eaten."

As usual, the music was blaring when they arrived. The local men avoided Rhonda, but were eyeing Ella as she entered. Gudrun also caught their attention. One big man stepped into Ella's path and arched an eyebrow at her. His friend at the table snickered. Ella gave him a melting smile and linked her arm through his.

He led her towards the back door. As she watched them go, Gudrun felt an arm slide around her waist. "What about you sugar, want to come out back with me and get a taste of a real man?"

"I'd love nothing better," she replied, a sexy purr in her voice.

As he led Gudrun away, Rhonda looked at Igor hopefully. "All right, my pretty bird, we will dance, but you will have to hold me up." A moment later, Bran and Kylie joined them on the dance floor. Once Ella and Gudrun had returned, they gathered at the table and ordered food.

The server set the food on the table then stopped and looked at Gudrun. "Oh, honey, looks like you've got a blood spot on your collar. That's going to be a bitch to get out. Here, let me try." She leaned closer and started dabbing at Gudrun's collar. "I know who you are," she whispered.

Gudrun's fierce blue eyes locked on her, holding her still. The girl just smiled innocently. "Come with me to the ladies, I think I can get that out for you." So saying, she took Gudrun by the arm and led her away.

The others looked at each other, concern etched on their faces. Gudrun followed the girl into the ladies room. The girl swiftly checked to make sure the room was empty then turned to Gudrun. "Listen, I don't know what department you're working for, but we've been working on this drug ring for months. We're getting nowhere because the local sheriff is in on it, blocking us at every turn. He went nuts a few days ago and your guys threw him in the clink. We had to bust him out.

"Now, I don't know what you told Gary to shut him up, but I really want to help, and I want these druggies out of business. Man in the far left corner as we leave this room, he's the main pusher, and we suspect him of making a number of people disappear. You're that merc, Gudrun Arielsdottir, you can make him disappear and no one can touch you for it.

"Also, the three men to his left are carrying guns, they're his bodyguards."

"They make people disappear?" said Gudrun.

"Yeah, they drag them out into the woods, then they don't come back, or so the story goes."

"Keep this to yourself," said Gudrun, "we'll deal with it, and soon. So, you a local cop?"

"On loan from Portland, my first assignment."

Gudrun nodded. "Okay, play along and we'll go back. Thanks for the intel."

The girl nodded, then Gudrun linked arms with her and led her back to the main room. "Thanks for getting that spot out for me, sugar. You're amazing."

She was smiling brightly as she sat facing Igor. He felt her eyes on him and looked up from his food. Gudrun's eyes went to the man alone first, then to the three others. Igor nodded that he understood. He nudged Bran's knee then nodded to Gudrun. He got the message. By this time Kylie and Ella had also clued in these four men were of interest. They finished their food then left the bar.

Later, as the bar closed, the four men exited, heading for a large SUV. As they neared, Igor stepped in their path, holding up his badge. "Excuse me, gentlemen, I have a few questions for you."

The three bodyguards went for their guns, but a voice from a distant hell stopped them cold. *"Freeze. Look at the sky and count to two hundred and fifty."* They looked up and began to count. Ella threw the drug dealer over her shoulder and marched away. He was still counting and trying to see the sky as she tossed him through the door of the motel room.

"Be silent. You will answer all questions put to you. You will answer truthfully. He's all yours, Igor."

"Thank you, Miss Ella. Miss Gudrun?"

Gudrun stepped up to the man. "You are a drug dealer, correct?"

"Sort of."

"Explain."

"I'm the supplier. I sell it to the dealers."

"You're the supplier for the sheriff, correct?" asked Igor.

"Yes."

Igor nodded to Gudrun, so she continued. "Do you sometimes take people into the forest and kill them?"

"No."

Gudrun thought for a moment. "Do you capture people and take them into the forest?"

"Yes."

"What do you do with them there?"

"Give them to the sheriff."

"Why?"

"So he can give them to her as a present."

"Who is she?"

"I don't know."

"What do you know of her?"

"She likes them fresh, still breathing."

"You will show us the place where you deliver the fresh ones."

"It's the freak camp on the way to the ghost town. I don't know where he takes them from there."

Gudrun turned to Igor and arched an eyebrow at him. "We'll take him to that place," said Igor, "tie him up and leave him where she can find him. We could get lucky."

"This is a task for Gudrun and I," said Ella. "You boys are pretty beat up, you need to rest."

"I'll go with you," said Rhonda. Ella arched an eyebrow at her. "Eye in the sky, independent scout, remember. I can let you know if anything is going sideways." Ella nodded and Rhonda leaped through the window before Igor could try to talk her out of it.

A short while later the hawk watched from above while the two vampires baited the trap. They tied the drug dealer to a tree, then released him from the compulsion. He began to shout and bluster, making threats and more. Gudrun went full vampire and bit his neck, allowing the blood to run. The man began to scream and beg.

Gudrun and Ella slipped into the trees and waited while the hawk circled lazily overhead. The air was chilly and, as time passed, they began to notice the cold. Their bait had long since stopped screaming and just hung limply from the ropes. Finally giving in to the chill creeping into their bones, Ella transformed and lay down.

"Sure, it's all fine for you to relax, you've got fur," Gudrun muttered, as the cat eyed her then returned its attention to the clearing where the scent of fresh blood was still on the air. She glanced up to see the hawk making a tight circle to the left. The prey was finally coming.

The small vampire was on full alert as she approached the familiar spot. The former sheriff, covered in dirt and leaves followed along, hoping for a kind word from his mistress, or perhaps a chance to persuade her to leave this area forever. It was too dangerous now, but she was hungry, so hungry.

As they drew nearer, her sense of impending danger grew stronger. She stopped and reached out with all her senses. There it was, the dangerous woman, and yet another. Every instinct she had told her to run away, but she was nearly mad with hunger. Using all the stealth she could muster she moved closer.

All at once she saw it through the trees, a body hanging from ropes in the clearing. It was still alive, but still the dangerous woman was near, and so was something else. Nothing moved and the hunger burned at her, overpowering the desire to flee. She moved closer.

With the speed of a striking cobra the vampire streaked from the shadows. The man screamed as his arms were torn from the sockets and his body jerked into the trees. She fastened her mouth on his bleeding neck even as she fled through the forest, carrying the body.

She'd been quick, but not quick enough, they were coming, fast. Gudrun bore down on her, but the former sheriff stepped into her path. The force of her body crashing into him hurled him against a tree where he sank to the ground, moaning, but it had been enough, she'd lost sight of the tiny vampire.

The small one wasn't home free yet. As she fled she saw movement in her peripheral vision and, dropping her prize, darted through a hole in an old tree. It was enough to cause the tigress to miss. Dodging around the tree Ella found a small hole in the ground, too small for her or Gudrun to enter. She transformed back to the woman as Gudrun arrived at the tree.

Gudrun grinned as she found Ella swearing like a sailor. "The little abomination has escaped me for the moment, but she has to come out of there sometime."

"Unless there's another way out," said Gudrun. "I'm betting there is. Slippery little shit, isn't she?"

"Yes," grumbled Ella, as the hawk spiraled down to them, "she certainly is. Ronni, did you see her come out anywhere?"

"I did," sighed Rhonda as she joined. "She came out about a hundred yards ahead almost as soon as she went in. Before I could get a marker circle going she was into another cave. There appears to be a network of caves around here. Ladies, you're not going to catch her this way now. You need the boys."

"Ronni, even Igor isn't a match for this one," said Gudrun.

"No, no, Gudrun, I mean you need them to track her. The wolves can track her, push her hard, never letting her rest. All you have to do is stay near them. Eventually they'll tire her, and she'll turn to fight. You two can work in shifts, one resting while the other hunts with the wolves."

"Gudrun?"

"Yes, Mother, the Lady Hawk is right. The wolves are our best bet for running her down now. Ronni, go back and bring the boys. Send Kylie with warm clothing for Ella as well. Tell her to get as close as she can, Ella will meet her then sleep in the car. When she's rested you can lead her to us and then I'll rest."

"There's no need to involve Kylie," said Ella. "I will rest in cat form."

"Then we have a plan. Go, Ronni," said Gudrun. "Ella and I will follow her scent until the wolves catch up." The hawk leaped into the sky and the vampires set out to find the trail of their prey.

DEEP IN A CAVERN, A small vampire sat amid a huge pile of bones, hugging a ragged doll to her breast. "That was too close, Maggie, too close. We did get something to eat, but not enough, we're still hungry. That dangerous woman turned into a monster, and she had another one with her. They tried to hurt us, Maggie, but we got away.

"They killed the carue, both of them. How could that happen? How could they kill the carue? Even we couldn't kill them. We'll have to go into the town to get something to eat, Maggie. Yes, I know it's dangerous, but we're hungry. We have to go to the town. I'll be careful, Maggie, I promise I will, and I'll come home with new fresh bones for you to play with. You stay here and keep watch.

BACK AT THE CASTLE, Marta was reading as Amanda approached. "Well, how are we enjoying this sunny Autumn day?" She got no response. Marta rose and wandered a short distance away to give Amanda and Larise some privacy to talk. "Larise? How are you feeling?"

"Okay, I guess."

"Still processing?"

"No, not really. Just don't really care anymore. Nothing matters."

"Oh? What doesn't matter?"

"Anything. Everything. I'm just numb inside, empty like I've been completely hollowed out. Nothing left but the empty shell."

"All right, let's try something else. What do you remember?"

"Everything. All of it."

"Okay, let's start with how you felt when Ella brought you out of the hospital room."

"How I felt?"

"Yes. What was it like, to suddenly regain your command of English, to be understood and believed?"

"Euphoric. It was like a building had been lifted off my shoulders. I was exhausted from fighting against the drugs they'd given me, and so thrilled that this beautiful and dangerous woman believed me."

"Dangerous? What made you use that word?"

"She is. Everything about her screams of danger. I was trained to sense dangerous situations and people. It was like a goddess had come to me, fixed me, or so we all believed. I was afraid of her, but worshiped her too."

"I can see that," smiled Amanda. "All right, let's move on to when you first arrived at the Lair. Tell me what that was like."

"I felt like Alice after falling down the rabbit hole. It was crazy, but Ella had told me it was okay and I'd be safe, so I just took it all in."

"What about when Igor assigned Branimir to be your bodyguard? How did that feel?"

"I was resistant, after all, I was a trained agent, why did I need a bodyguard? In spite of myself I was attracted to him, but old trust issues wouldn't let me show that, or enjoy it."

"Let's explore some of that, Larise. You were attracted to him. How did you feel about it after a couple of days?"

Larise studied her hands for a moment. Finally she sighed. "I liked it, a lot, but wouldn't admit it to myself, wouldn't let it show. For a while I thought ..."

"Yes?"

"The carue had taken me over. They said I tried to kill Kylie, but I have no memory of that. Bran put his arms around me and Igor said he wasn't going to kill Bran's girl. I made a fuss about that title, but in truth, I liked it, wanted it to be real."

"What did it feel like?"

"Warm, it felt warm, and safe. I wanted to stay in his arms, but the carue destroyed that."

"Oh? Tell me?"

"I guess you'll find out anyway."

"Larise, you have doctor/patient privilege here. You can speak freely. Tell me what happened."

"The carue took me over again. They told me I cracked Bran over the head with a gun and ran away. They say I shot and killed the Lady Hawk, but I have no real memory of that.

"I came to in the forest, so weak I couldn't stand. Apparently I shot Igor too, but only wounded him. He tried to kill me, but Bran got in his face and so did Ella. Lady Hawk revived and Igor went to find food for her.

"Lady Hawk then ordered Ella to drink most of my blood so I'd be helpless. I know she wanted to kill me herself, but Ella wouldn't allow it.

"Bran told me all this as he held me by the throat. He said I'd broken his trust, his heart, and destroyed his place in his pack. He said Igor would kill him for the challenge when he tried to defend me. I tried to reach out, but he slapped my hand away and said he didn't want me near him again. They dragged me back and here I am."

"You have no emotional attachment to any of this?"

"None. I'm just empty inside. Nothing."

"Not even when you think of Branimir's anger?"

"No. He said I'd broken his heart, and at the time, that broke mine, but now ... nothing."

"Nothing at all?"

"No. Would it be all right if I went for a walk to the farmhouse and back?"

"Of course, Larise. I'll send Marta back to you."

Amanda walked away, stopping to speak with Marta for a moment. Larise showed no signs of surprise when the girl shimmered into a dire wolf and approached her. She started off toward the farmhouse in the distance, the wolf trotting along behind her. These people didn't trust her either, she could tell; nor should they.

AMANDA FOUND THE QUEEN watching from the doorway. "Amanda?"

"I can't discuss specifics, but the woman is utterly bereft of all emotion. Either the death of the carue has truly destroyed her ability to feel, or it will suddenly all come crashing back and destroy her. Sally, any insights you could share with me would help immensely."

"I'll do a reading for her later and let you know if anything appears for me."

The Hunt Goes On

Ella caught the scent first and the two vampires set out in pursuit of the prey. While they searched and cursed when they found it entered a cave too small for them, the tiny killer was already on her way to the town of Tanner's Ridge, slipping easily through the night.

Gudrun gave a shout and the tigress came to her. "She came out here, we have the scent again." The tigress trotted ahead of her, following the scent, but was soon stymied by yet another narrow cave. This one went straight into the side of the mountain. The great cat snarled and shimmered back into the woman.

"Curse that tiny abomination," snarled Ella.

Gudrun nodded thoughtfully. "I think I know why the carue had so many enthralled animals. You said most of them were small, foxes, weasels, and such."

"Yes. This has puzzled me, what do you think their main purpose was?"

"I think they were either tracking or watching the vampire. I think the carue and the vampire were at odds, and yet shared a hunting ground. The vampire probably tried to kill the carue, but wasn't strong enough."

"And the second carue?" asked Ella. "Who knows, another of Mobutu's, the tiny vampire's maybe. There could be more of them."

"I agree. I also believe that, if there are, they'll be in this general area. Once we dispose of this little bugger we'll need Igor's whole pack. They can sweep this entire area, clean out whatever's left."

"I believe this idea is wise," sighed Ella, "but we'll have to stay with them in case they encounter another vampire."

Gudrun nodded her agreement as the Lady Hawk spiraled down. The two wolves joined them, each carrying a bottle of blood strapped around their neck. "She went in there," said Rhonda. "I can go hawk and get in there, none of you can get close."

"No, Sweet Ronni," said Igor.

"It's the only way, sweetheart. I'm the only one who'll fit."

"No, I forbid it ..."

"You forbid?" bristled the Lady Hawk. "You forbid?"

"Easy, little sister," chuckled Gudrun, "you can beat him up later. Right now we need him. Igor's right, Ronni, sure you can fit in there, but if you get caught, you'll be killed. You're no match for a vampire in tight quarters. You're a creature of the open skies."

Rhonda was looking at her, fire in her eyes. "Listen, my savage sister," grinned Gudrun, "we need you alive. Look, we know this little monster always has a bolt hole. Igor and Bran can sniff that out, Ella can go with them. I'll settle in here in case she comes out this way. If she's made a getaway you can come back for me, and we'll take up the trail again."

Somewhat mollified, Rhonda nodded her acquiescence. Shaking a warning finger at Igor she leaped into the sky and vanished into the morning sun. Ella ruffled Igor's hair. "That was an unfortunate choice of words, my young friend."

"Da," he sighed. "I have serious sucking up to do. Come on Bran, let's go find a vampire to annoy, safer than facing the angry Lady Hawk." Branimir snickered as he shimmered back into the wolf. They sniffed around for a moment to get the scent then they set out.

Hours of hard ground covered later, the wolf howl alerted the two resting vampires. A cry from above had them looking up. The hawk wheeled once then led the way. Moving through the forest as quickly as they dared, the two vampires soon sighted the wolves. The trail was leading downhill. It didn't take long to realize the hungry vampire was headed for the town.

The wolves gave it up and raced on ahead, they'd realized where it was going. Ella and Gudrun struggled to keep them in sight while the hawk flew on ahead. They arrived at the motel to find the windows open and fresh clothing waiting for them. Ella dressed swiftly then she and Gudrun set out again, they could both sense the vampire near.

Igor transformed for only a moment. "Sweet Ronni."

"Yes?" was the cold response.

He sighed and allowed his shoulders to slump. "Sweet Ronni, I spoke wrongly to you, I fucked up, but there is need for haste. Can I suck up later?"

She fought to keep the grin from reaching her lips, but failed. "All right, buddy, but you're not off the hook yet." Merriment was dancing in her eyes and a smile at her lips. "What's the plan?"

"That thing is close. Go up and search, we'll hunt as wolf, staying out of sight. Miss Ella and Gudrun can move through the town. Kylie, get in the car and drive away until we call."

"Nu-uh," replied Kylie. "I've got weapons and I'm staying right here."

"I tried," growled Igor, as he shimmered into the wolf and leaped through the window. Bran was already outside and the hawk in the air.

While Ella and Gudrun grew frustrated trying to find a way through the caves and the hawk returned for the wolves, the small vampire cautiously made her way toward the town. As she drew nearer she threw caution to the wind and raced to the one place she knew she'd find prey, the back door of the bar.

That area was empty for the moment so she began to circle around to the edge of the parking lot. Reaching out with her senses she sought for the dangerous woman and her companion, but they were nowhere near. It was safe to hunt. It took a while, but eventually she saw what she wanted. A couple staggered out of the bar and towards their car. She stepped into their path.

"Look, it's a little girl," said the man. "Hey there, sweetheart, are you lost? You look like you've been out in the woods for a while. What's your name?"

"Emily."

"Where do you live, Emily?" asked the woman.

"I don't know."

"Tell you what," said the man. "You get in the back seat of the car, and we'll take a drive around, see if you can recognize your street, okay?"

"Okay. Thank you."

"Oh, that's all right, sweetie," said the woman, as she tucked the child in the back seat. Neither of them noticed the sly smile on the child's face nor the look of the predator in her eyes.

The motel, bar, gas station, store, and a couple of houses were a short way out of the main part of town. As soon as the car reached a lonely stretch of road she attacked, grabbing the driver's hair and dragging his head back over the seat, sinking her needle-sharp fangs into his neck and drinking noisily. The car swerved and the driver screamed as she took him.

The car crashed into a tree, but she didn't release her hold until he was dead and the blood no longer pumped into her mouth. The woman had managed to crawl out of, and away from the car, but the vampire soon found her. She swiftly met the same fate as her companion.

Once she was fully sated, the vampire started carrying the body of the woman into the forest, calling the former sheriff to her. She could feel him and he was still alive, functional. He could help carry the body back to the cave.

The wolves found the scent and followed it to the parking lot, but lost it again where the vampire had boarded the car. Joining them,

Gudrun cursed while they waited for Ella to arrive. "So, what now?" asked Ella.

"Someone took her away in a car," said Gudrun. "She was probably pretending to be a lost child. Now I guess it'll be up to Kylie to locate her, or her rescuer."

"No," replied Ella. "This thing is completely feral. It wouldn't wait long before feeding. We'll probably find that car off the road nearby with a dead body in it. Go on, boys, find that car."

The two wolves raced away, sticking to the shadows at the side of the road. Gudrun and Ella set out after them. It wasn't long until they heard the howl of the hunting wolf. Just as Ella predicted, the car was against a tree, the driver dead behind the wheel. His throat had been torn out and he was drained of blood.

"Dammit," snarled Ella, "now what do we do?"

"I'll deal with this," said Gudrun. "You three get on her trail, I'll catch up."

Ella nodded and the wolves set out with the tigress trotting along beside. Gudrun scooped up Ella's clothes, then found a rag in the car, stuffed it in the gas tank, and set it afire. A Few minutes later the tank exploded. The body would be too badly burned to notice that it had been drained of blood. She set out after the hunters.

THE QUEEN SIGHED DEEPLY and leaned against the king's shoulder. "Their quarry is elusive, Harald my love, elusive and deadly. It's killed two people and has carried off the woman's body. The wolves are tracking her now and Ella's with them. Gudrun is cleaning up the mess she left behind.

"I believe they will eventually succeed. The mountainous terrain is the real hindrance for them now. The small one is all too familiar with the area, but our people have one advantage the vampire is unaware of."

"Oh?"

"The Lady Hawk. Harald, Ronni is quickly becoming one of our greatest assets."

"But still something about her troubles you?"

"Yes and no. Ronni is utterly devoted to Igor, and to us for that matter. She is also becoming a strong leader."

"But she's wild as a hawk?"

"Yes, that," chuckled Sally. "Exactly that. The girl is a real independent thinker. Then there's the problem of Larise."

"Ah yes, what to do about Larise. A woman with her training would be an asset, that's for certain, but with the state she's in now she's of no use to us, and we can't send her back, not now."

"Harald?"

"She knows too much about us, far too much. We can't compel it out of her, it's too dangerous, and we can't trust her."

"Harald, you can't kill her," gasped Sally.

He reached and gently pulled her close again. "What's the alternative, imprison her for the rest of her life? Would that be any kinder than a swift death? Show me another way that will ensure her loyalty and assure me that we have her trust."

Sally sighed and snuggled closer. "Please give me some time to think about this, lover. There must be a way, there must."

"All right, sweet Sally, if anyone can find a way it's you. I'm in no hurry to murder the girl, trust me on that. We'll give it until Igor tidies up that mess out west before making any final decisions. Get some rest now, my precious girl. Perhaps the answer will come in dreams."

While Queen Sally drifted off to sleep, a watchful werewolf sat reading, yet keeping an eye on the woman who just stood staring out the window. She spent many hours each day watching while the woman stared out the window, walked the fields, watched the cows, slowly and carefully weeded a flower garden, but the air was growing colder and that pastime would soon be finished for the year.

Perhaps today would be a good day to take her back to the library. Marta needed a new book to read and some lively conversation.

Monster on the Run

The wolves moved confidently through the forest, the trail easy to follow. The mighty tigress paced along beside them, her mind fixed on the prey now. This was a hunt she was familiar with. How many times in the past had she relentlessly tracked down a rogue vampire? It was easier when it was one of her own creations for her ties to it would lead her to her prey, but not with Terga's line. Those took time to hunt down and destroy, but destroy it she would.

High overhead the hawk soared, keen eyes seeking, searching, relentless as the wolves and tigress below. She noted the general direction of the wolf's travel and flew on ahead in ever widening circles. Suddenly she saw movement, something huge, awkward, and struggling. A tight bank, circle back, and bingo.

Down below, in the gloom of pre-dawn, was the former sheriff, struggling up the mountainside carrying the body of a dead woman. The vampire was nowhere in sight, but she had to be close. The hawk turned back and dropped down to meet up with the wolves.

She swooped in low and transformed in midair, dropping to the moss in an easy three-point landing. "Now that was truly impressive," grinned Igor who had transformed as soon as he saw her closing in, "a perfect super hero landing by a beautiful naked woman. I'm hopelessly in love now."

"God, you suck up nice," grinned Rhonda. "Igor, up ahead our friend, the former sheriff, is carrying the body of a dead woman. The vampire has to be near."

"Lead on, magical lady."

"Save some of that charm until I get you alone."

She laughed as she leaped into the air and flew away, the wolves and tigress following as best they could. The day was growing light as they caught up with the man carrying the grisly load. Catching sight of them he dropped his burden and pulled out a gun. "Get away," he shouted as he fired at the wolves. "Get away, she doesn't want you here. Get away."

They were all stunned at what happened next. Without warning the hawk stooped. She dropped from the sky like a stone, banked at the last second, transformed and slammed into him from behind. The man was knocked to the ground unconscious, while the Lady Hawk rolled easily to her feet then leaped skyward again with a piercing cry.

With a groan the man returned to consciousness. Back in human form Igor hauled him to his feet and slammed him against a tree. "Please, you have to go away, she doesn't want you here. She'll hurt me, please, just go away."

"If we go away can you find her?"

"Yes. Yes, I can find mistress. She wants fresh bones to play with. I have to take them to her secret place. Just go away."

"All right, since you ask so nicely, we'll go away, but first you have to talk to her."

Igor roughly shoved the man towards Ella. *"Pay attention. We left, returned to the town. You are not being followed. Quickly now, return to your mistress."* Without a word the former sheriff gathered up the body of the dead woman and set out again with the two wolves and tigress following closely.

"They're coming, Maggie, I can feel them. He's leading them right to our home. I'm so sorry Maggie, but we have to leave and find a new place to hide. These evil people will never leave us alone. First we have to kill him though. He can feel us and will lead them right to us. We'll make a new one when we find a new home.

"Come on, Maggie, you have to come with me. We'll kill him then we'll hide until they go to sleep then we'll leave to find a new home. I can't leave you here, Maggie, they might find you then I'd be all alone. Come on, let's go." So saying, she tucked the ragged doll into the torn and blood spattered jacket and set out.

The man carrying the corpse neared what looked like a cave in the rock face, completely ignoring the three creatures following close behind him. Without warning something streaked from the trees, blood spattered everywhere and the man crumpled to the ground making choking sounds. His attacker had already vanished down into another cave.

Igor was still swearing when Rhonda reached the ground and transformed. "Did you see where the little fucker came out?"

"Yes, my love, the little fucker came out about twenty yards that way then disappeared into yet another cave. She's in the caves again."

"This is taking too long," sighed Igor. "We need a better plan. This cave looks big enough to get into, maybe something is in there that will help us."

"All right, lover, you check it out, I'll go up and keep an eye out for the sneaky little critter."

Rhonda leaped skyward and Igor turned and led the way cautiously into the cave. What they found nearly made him sick. There were human bones everywhere, most still wearing a semblance of clothing.

"They're in pairs," mused Ella, as she gazed all around at the piles of bones.

"Pairs?"

"Yes, Igor, pairs, male and female mostly. See there? I think, in her twisted mind, she's trying to re-create her parents."

"Seriously?

"Imagine the trauma to a young mind to see the death of her family, to be ravished and drained of blood then left at the mercy of the thirst. The line of Mobutu has always been insane, the change being too great for their minds to handle, also the savage and brutal manner of their change. It's much easier for those who are wanting the change and it's done in a truly loving way. Even then it's rare for someone to survive it with a whole mind."

"Da, you're right, Miss Ella. Killing this thing will be a kindness to it," said Branimir.

"Yes it will," agreed Ella. "Poor child. Damn Mobutu, his evil lives on long after he died."

"We will find and stop this one, Miss Ella," said Igor. "Then we have a big mess to clean up. Get rid of the bodies, explain away the deaths, clear the area of changed animals, Kylie has her work cut out for her."

"Yes, this will challenge even her abilities with bullshit," grinned Ella. "I wish I had a phone so I could check in."

"Here, use mine," said Gudrun, as she entered the cave. "So, we found the den, but she got away?"

Igor sighed. "Da."

"Hey, it happens, don't let it get to you. Stay focused on the job." He nodded as she slapped his shoulder and walked outside where Ella was admonishing Kylie to be careful. Igor and Bran were close behind, and then the Hawk called from above. She was wheeling to the left. They set out at a run.

WHILE THE HUNTERS TRIED to chase down the elusive child vampire, Larise sat in the library, talking to Torvil Reyburne, the librarian. "It truly grieves me," he sighed. She looked up at him, but didn't speak. This man from an ancient world would surely have piqued her curiosity before, but not now. "You," he smiled. "It grieves me to see so beautiful a woman completely disinterested in life."

"Sorry," she said, shrugging her shoulders.

"Dear girl, how did you come to this pass?"

"You already know."

"I know that you're a highly trained agent, and you don't get there without displaying some drive and ambition. I also know you encountered a carue, and inadvertently got marked by it. I've also come to know what that mark can mean. Will you forgive me if I ask someone else to join us for a moment?"

"Huh? Oh, sure."

Torvil took out his phone and hit the button. A quick scan gave him the desired number and he called. It was answered on the third ring. "Sawchuk."

"Terry, it's Torvil. I hear your good wife is away on a mission."

"Yup, she went west without me."

"Hard times, brother, hard times. Do you have a few minutes to spare for me?"

"Sure, what's up."

"I need you in the library, can you come?"

"On my way."

Torvil sighed as he closed the connection and dropped the phone back into his coat pocket. The fact that he was a caveman dressed in the style of the Victorian Era didn't seem to fizz on Larise Parker, neither did she show any interest in why he'd called Terry Sawchuk. He gazed at her sadly.

A few minutes later, Terry arrived and pulled up a chair. "So, what's up, Torvil?"

"It's Larise. You know what happened."

"Yeah, I do. Larise, what happened to you really sucks and I wish I could make it better for you, but I can't."

"Don't be so sure."

"Torvil?"

"Terry, Larise got marked by a vampire, a carue, but marked none-the-less. The carue was killed and now she's left to deal with the loss of that bond, no matter how badly she didn't want it. You're the only other human I know of who's been marked and lost that connection, however briefly. Of us all, you're the only one who can relate to what she's going through."

Terry nodded. "Yeah, I guess I can at that." He turned his full attention to Larise. "Gudrun marked me and then left on assignment. On that assignment she was killed and her body disposed of. It took days to get her back, and for those few days I was as empty as you are now. I know how you feel, and it truly sucks."

"How did you manage?" she asked, finally showing a bit of interest.

"I worked up a burning hate for the man who killed her, and I fed it constantly."

"I wish I could do that, but I hated that thing and I'm glad it's dead, but ..."

"You're still empty inside," sighed Terry. "I get that."

Torvil still looked thoughtful. "Terry, can you tell me what it felt like when she revived and the connection was re-established?"

"Wow, hard to describe. Everything came back in a rush. Her charred body gave a lurch and she drew breath, and so did I for the first time in days. I felt the life, the fire of my whole being, come rushing back. I was filled with life again, I was me again, I was whole again."

Torvil nodded, his mind racing, then he rose to his feet. "You folks wait here; I shouldn't be long." With that he walked away.

Puzzled, Terry looked at Larise, then Marta, then shrugged. Marta passed him a book and he relaxed back into his chair.

Torvil found the king and queen in their private study. "What's on your mind, Torvil?" asked King Harald.

"Queen Sally, did you tell the king I was looking for him?"

"I did," she laughed, as she indicated he should sit. "Nothing gets past you, does it? So, what's on your mind?"

"Larise."

"I'll admit that one's got us stumped, Torvil," sighed the king. "I've never encountered anything like this before. Usually it's the marked one who passes from age. We mourn them, but it doesn't destroy us the way it has her. She should be rejoicing that the damn thing is dead, but instead she's bereft of all desire for life."

"Yes. I've been putting some thought into this, and I think I may have the solution."

"You do?" Both the king and queen sat up straighter and looked at him eagerly. "Well, don't just sit there, tell us," said the queen.

"Well, the mark creates a bond, an unbreakable bond. It also seems to tie the markee to the marker in other ways as well, not necessarily a love bond, but a need to serve the one who marked them above all else. Sire, you marked the house staff, did you not?"

"I did."

"Why?"

"To ensure their loyalty."

"And in return for that?"

"They get my protection, a place for life, safety, ... what are you driving at, Torvil?"

"Do you deliberately instill that bargain when you mark them, or is it intrinsic to the mark?"

"It's intrinsic to the mark. Torvil?"

"Bear with me now. So, Larise was marked, unwittingly, but marked none-the-less, and so she was compelled to serve that which marked her, even against her will. With that suddenly torn away from her, that one reason she had to exist, she was left as we now know her, lost, bereft, uncaring.

"Sire, before that thing marked her she was a dedicated agent, a woman with a purpose, a desire to serve, a reason to live."

"Yes, but, do you believe the carue's mark supplanted her prior reason to live?"

"I do."

"So, what's the solution?"

"Harald, I believe that, if you mark her as you have the others, you will restore her, give her a new reason to live, to serve. She's a bright young woman and she has the training for this life."

Stunned, the king just looked at Torvil. Sally gripped her husband's arm tightly. "Harald, he's got it. That's the solution, the answer. Her reason to live was yanked away, but you can give that back, and more, once she carries your mark she could always be trusted. Lover, you always say the simplest solutions are often the best."

King Harald reached out and gripped Torvil's shoulder. "My friend, how I do love the way that mind of yours works. You could be right about this. Is she in the library right now?"

"I believe so," grinned Torvil.

"Well then, let's go. If she's willing we'll give this a try." All three rose and headed for the library.

The king, queen, and Torvil arrived to find Terry and Marta reading, and Larise sitting quietly, staring at her hands. They started to rise, but the king indicated they should sit. At the king's nod, Torvil explained his idea and his reasoning.

"So, you think this will restore me?" asked Larise, showing a small glimmer of interest.

"We do," replied Torvil.

"This will be your decision to make, Larise," said the king, as he took her hands gently. "I won't hurt you, but, you will be bound to me for the rest of your life if we do this."

"What will happen to me, will you take me over and make me do things like the carue did?"

"No girl, never that. Actually, as a highly skilled agent, you would be a great asset to us. You would work for me as do the others."

"You mean like that girl who always brings stuff before you know you want it."

"Elaine, yes, like that, except that Elaine is household staff by her own choice. I assume you would prefer to serve as a field agent."

"Could I do that? How could you or any of the others ever trust me after what I've done? I might betray you again."

"No you won't," grinned Harald. "Once I put my mark on you, you will be utterly devoted to me and my kingdom. You will become the most loyal and trustworthy agent in my employ."

"So, I'll fall in love with you like Terry did with Gudrun? I'll be ..."

"No girl, not quite, but you will like me a lot, and you will always be eager to please me. Larise, I swear to you, I have never, in over fourteen centuries of life, ever abused a servant, a marked assistant. I prefer to think of myself as more of a grandfather figure to my staff."

Tears began to leak from her eyes as she felt emotion returning after so long. "I think I'd prefer to think of you as my king. Sire, would I be free to love another?"

"Of course you would, Larise. I won't put a lover's mark on you. So, still got a thing for Branimir?"

"I'm afraid he'll kill me on sight. Ah well, it's worth the risk, I can't go on like this. I've told you people several times to kill me because I can't be trusted, and you haven't. Maybe this way you will actually be able to trust me."

"We'll trust you completely, and you will be worthy of that trust."

Larise closed her eyes and took a deep breath. "Okay, do it. I don't want to live like this any longer."

King Harald shifted in his chair to move closer to her. "Relax, take long deep breaths." He extended his fangs and made a small bite on his wrist. "Now, Larise, taste my blood, just a taste, that's all you need."

Haltingly, she gazed fearfully into his eyes as she lowered her lips to his wrist. He smiled as he felt her tongue flick across his skin. She pulled back and he lifted her wrist to his lips. Gazing into her eyes, he bit her just enough to break the skin. He took a small taste of her blood then licked the wound on her arm to seal it.

He was still holding her eyes. "Larise Parker, I claim you as my own, you're mine now, and as long as I live no other can claim you, command you, or compel you against your will." He gave her hand a gentle squeeze then released it.

Tears sprang from her eyes and her body began to shake with the power of the returning emotions. She was instantly in Sally's arms. "Oh my god, oh my dear sweet god."

"Easy, Larise," cooed Sally. "Take your time. This can be a bit emotional."

"I'm alive again. I can't explain it, but I feel whole again. Oh god, what I did ..."

"That was the carue," said the king, "not you. From this moment on, what you do will be you and I together. Look at me, Larise, you can feel it, can't you."

"Yes, oh yes. Oh god, that was so gentle, yet I could feel it. You said look at me and I felt a great desire to do so. King Harald, is this what's it's like?"

"Yes, my girl, it is. That other was basically an animal's desires, a beast's commands and desires. Now, you take a few days to get settled again then we'll sit down together and see how it's working for you."

"Sire, how can I ever thank you for restoring me. You have no idea what this means to me."

"Actually I do," he grinned, "for I can feel you too. You take the day and play now, Larise. I have other things to do."

Larise suddenly sat up straighter with wide eyes. "Sword practice."

"That's right," he smiled. "Sword practice." With that he took Sally's arm and together they walked away.

IGOR AND COMPANIONS arrived at the cliff edge to find Ronni sitting on a boulder by a waterfall. "Ronni? Tell me she didn't."

"She did," sighed the Lady Hawk. "She didn't even hesitate. I was circling above when she saw the cliff and picked up speed until she hit open space. She splatted on the rocks below, but has already revived and gone into the trees."

"She'll be hungry, kill anything that moves until she gets her fill. If we can get down into that ravine we'll probably find her still there, hunting," said Gudrun.

"She doesn't escape me that easy," snarled Igor. "This one doesn't know the Russian wolves."

"Da," agreed Branimir. "When we hunt, we hunt until we kill the prey, no matter how long that takes." Both men shimmered into wolf form and started down the steep hillside, searching for a way across the ravine.

The two vampires followed as best they could, their admiration for the werewolves growing steadily. "Damn," muttered Gudrun, as she scrambled down the steep incline, "I sure wouldn't want those guys on my trail." For an answer, the saber-toothed cat hurried past her.

They approached a narrow spot about halfway down. The wolves stopped to gauge their chances, but with a roar of challenge the tigress sped past them and leaped into open space. She landed on the opposite side and slipped into the trees.

With a snarl of frustration, Igor continued on down the hill, Branimir and Gudrun close behind. None of them could have made that leap. Igor finally reached the bottom and crossed the tumbling cascade. They headed back up the hill, searching for either Ella's scent or the vampire's.

High overhead the Lady Hawk constantly searched the terrain below. Nothing escaped her attention, no movement, no matter how small, passed unnoticed. Finally she saw it, the tiny vampire perched in a tree over a game trail. Below on the trail paced the hunting tigress.

The hawk screamed a warning but it was too late, the small killer dropped down onto the tiger's back and bit deep. The young vampire had no idea what she'd attacked. Even as she landed and bit, the huge cat was moving. Hurling herself beneath a low hanging branch, the tigress scraped off her tiny attacker.

The small vampire was lightning quick and leaped back on the attack, but she met a huge paw coming the other way and was hurled well back to strike hard against a rock face. The big cat leaped at her, but the diminutive monster managed to scramble away and wriggle into tumbled rocks where the cat couldn't reach her.

With the tigress pacing back and forth, searching for a way through the jumble of stone to the small vampire inside, the young one searched for a way out. Whimpering in fear, she continued to flinch away each time a huge paw reached through, searching for a hold on her. Suddenly she found what appeared to be an animal burrow and she eagerly wriggled into the tunnel.

It was a tight squeeze, but she managed to reach a larger room. The darkness was deep, but her enhanced vision allowed her to explore. A low growl of warning reached her. The vampire spun around and put her back to the wall, she knew that scent, she was in a badger's den, but it was a wolverine she faced.

Wolverines were tough prey, and this was a tight place to fight one, but she was also hungry. As the beast took a step toward her she snarled and hurled herself at it.

The battle was short and bloody, but she prevailed and drank all of its blood. It was enough to heal her, but not enough to slake her thirst. Her search for a second way out was rewarded and she slipped away while the great cat and companions sat waiting for her to reappear. The tunnel led out near the rushing river and the sound of the water hid her escape.

Darkness fell and slowly faded onto dawn before Igor transformed back into the man. He raised his arm and the hawk dropped from the sky to transform and land beside him. "She's gone," he sighed, as he put an arm around Rhonda.

Ella and Branimir had transformed as well. "Da, her scent is growing colder. Do you smell the other, Igor?"

"Badger. She must have found a badger's den with another way out."

"We've lost her trail for now," said Gudrun. "We're done here, people. Let's find a road where a car can reach us. I'll call Kylie for a ride. We need to rest, and we need to eat.

"Igor, you can call the king and report." Gudrun reached out to grip his arm. "Igor, it's okay. You can't win them all, and this little monster is slippery as the one who made her."

"Mobutu."

"Yes," said Ella. "That man was as elusive as a wisp of smoke, but Gudrun eventually cornered him. This will be difficult, but we will track her down."

"Yes, we will," said Igor.

"Igor?"

"We'll find her trail, Bran and me. You folks go back and rest, we'll find the trail and follow her."

"No, my young friend," smiled Ella, "we like you and want to keep you alive. Yes, you beat the carue, but this one is stronger and faster. We all need rest."

"Wolves on the hunt never rest," growled Igor, as he and Branimir transformed and began searching for the scent. Ella just shook her head as they made wider and wider circles until Bran gave a yap and set out, Igor racing to catch up.

"Yeah, they're like that," grinned Rhonda. "Once Igor gets on a trail neither hell nor high water will stop him. Let's go, ladies." With that she leaped skyward and followed the direction the wolves had taken.

The scent was easy to follow and the wolves were running as the trail led downhill. They soon found the carcass of a deer, it had been drained of blood. They ran on, but eventually reached the highway and lost the scent at the roadside. The vampire had managed to hitch a ride. She was gone.

Gudrun and Ella caught up and sat beside the dejected wolves and hawk. They were just inside the tree line, watching the traffic speed by. Gudrun called Kylie for a ride, and they sat waiting for her to arrive.

"She caught a ride, I take it."

"Yes, Miss Gudrun, we lost the scent there. She's headed south."

"You sure about that Igor?"

"Da, I am. That side of the road faces south. She's feral, a child who has survived in the forest, she will avoid the cities, but will most likely find a small town near the forest and establish a new den. Only Kylie can put us back on the scent now."

While they waited for a ride back to the motel and a meal, the vampire sat beneath a tree far away, rocking back and forth as she hugged the remains of her ragged doll to her breast. The body of a huge man lay beside her.

Return to Duty

As King Harald neared the castle's exercise area, he heard someone working the heavy bag. He grinned as he recognized Larise's energy. "Good morning, Larise," he said, as he stepped through the door.

She stopped and dropped to one knee. "Good morning, Sire."

"Rise and relax, girl. There's no need to be so formal in here. You're back to your old self, I see."

"Better than ever before, my king," she replied, as she stood and removed the light gloves, tossing them onto the gym bag that sat near the heavy bag.

"What is it, Larise?"

"Sire, all my life I've been trying to prove myself, to my father, my teachers, instructors, supervisors, etc. Always trying to be worthy, to earn my place. Always trying to get people to see past my looks. Never at any time did I ever feel I had fully measured up."

"And now?"

"Now I feel different. I feel like I'll be even better at my job because I won't have to think about proving myself, I can focus on doing the job to the best of my ability. I don't have to think about the rest. I have my place; I've been accepted.

"Sire, there's no doubt in my mind you'd have made an end of me, or locked me away if you didn't think I had value to you, to your people. You didn't do that, instead you claimed me, restored me, accepted me, and now I'm ready to serve."

The king chuckled at that. "In a hurry, are you?"

"I've always been a bit of an eager beaver," she grinned. "Can't help it."

"All right, if you believe you're ready, I'll send you back into the field. Give me an hour, then meet me in the great hall." With a bright smile of delight, she fairly danced out of the gym and ran to her room. Elaine was waiting with her travel clothes freshly laundered and repaired. Her weapons were also lying beside the clothes.

"Elaine?"

"I thought you might be needing these."

"How do you do that?"

"I have no real idea, I just know. So, the king marked you too."

"Yes. God, it was like he brought me back from the dead. Was it like that for you too?"

"Sort of. It's my nature to serve, it's just what I do. I joined a BDSM club thinking I could find someone there to serve who would understand, but was a bad choice. I made a few more bad choices before I managed to wrangle an interview here.

"As soon as I learned what this place was, what I would be doing here, and that I would be marked, claimed forever, I knew this was it, it was right for me. Once the king marked and claimed me I felt settled inside, I'd found the place where I truly belong."

"The king and queen consider you their greatest treasure, Elaine."

"And I'm thrilled to be so. Now, how about you?"

"I can't explain it. What that animal did to me changed me forever, and not in a good way. Once it was killed, I was lost, soulless, empty inside, everything that I'd been before that incident was gone. Basically, Larise Parker was dead.

"When the king marked me, claimed me, I came alive again, inside. I feel like me again, but more settled, and now I have a purpose in life again, to serve the king, the king and his people, my people. Even better, I now have a friend who fully understands what it's like. You tried to tell me before, but I didn't understand, now I do. We're sisters now."

"Yes, we are," smiled Elaine. "Now, sister, the king is on his way to the great hall. I'll pack this for you, you go get your next assignment."

Excited, Larise kissed her cheek then fled to the great hall. She met Harald at the door, and he quirked an eyebrow at her. "Elaine told me you were coming," she grinned.

"Elaine, between her and Queen Sally, there's no place for me to hide," he chuckled, as he ushered her into the hall. He took his favorite chair and indicated she should sit near him.

There were a few other people there, as usual, but they continued with their own tasks. "All right, Larise, here's your assignment. I'm sending you back to Oregon."

Her eyes opened wide at that and she swallowed hard, but nodded her acquiescence. "Yes, Sire."

"I understand this is going to be difficult, but Ella and Gudrun will fully understand, and they will make sure Igor does as well. I'll call ahead to let them know you're coming. Larise, this isn't a punishment, nor is it a test of your loyalty, of these things I am utterly certain.

"No, this is for the werewolves, they need to know what has happened, they need to see firsthand the difference in you and what that means. It will also help them understand the level of devotion of any human the young vampire may claim to help her. I need for you and the wolves to be able to work together, and I need for them to trust that. Will you do this for me?"

"You're giving me a choice?"

"Yes, I am, girl. If you'd rather save this reunion for a later date I can find something else for you."

"No, Sire, you're right, I have to face them someday. We might as well get this resolved sooner rather than later. I'll go."

"That's the ticket. Eric ..."

"On my way, Sire," grinned the big man. "Warming up the plane."

Smiling, Harald nodded to Larise and she fled the hall. A few hours later she was back in Oregon, picking up a rental car.

THE HUNTERS ARRIVED back at the motel to find a strange car parked in front of Igor's room, and the door slightly ajar. Warily, they pushed the door open to see Larise sitting on the bed. "How did you get here?" asked Igor, as he stepped toward her flexing his hands menacingly.

"You have messages on your phone," she replied, as she tossed it to him. "You should check them now."

Igor gave her a hard look then turned on his phone and called up the first message. "Igor, it's King Harald. I've sent Larise back to you; I've marked and claimed her now. Ella or Gudrun can explain fully what that means. Report in as soon as you get this."

"The others are from the king too," said Larise. "At least I believe they all are."

"Aw crap," muttered Igor, as he hit the button and waited for the phone to ring.

"Harald here."

"Sire, it's Igor. You've sent Larise back to us. Do you believe that is safe to do?"

"Utterly certain. Igor, I understand what happened there, but I need you to keep a cool head and think this through. I've marked and claimed her, Ella can tell you what that means. Igor, I need you to be able to work with Larise."

"It will be as you desire, my king," sighed Igor. "In truth, another agent will be an asset."

"The young vampire got away from you, did she?"

"Da, she did. She escaped onto the highway and someone has given her a ride."

"Can you find her?"

"I believe so, Sire. She recently revived and will be hungry. She is also a creature of the forest, so she won't go far. We'll comb the area until we pick up the scent again."

"Igor, do you need more people?"

"Sire, I believe we can do this."

"You need to talk to Ella," chuckled the king. "She can tell you, sometimes tracking down a vampire takes a long time. Marlene once spent two years tracking a human through the northern forests. Take whatever time you need. The main thing is to keep all knowledge of what she is away from the humans."

"Understood, Sire."

"All right, I'll leave you to it." With that, he was gone.

Igor sighed and lowered the phone, gazing at Larise. "What happened?"

"You must have killed the carue."

"We did."

"That left me empty, soulless, dead but still walking. Apparently, once marked by a vampire, any type of vampire, a human can't truly exist as more than an empty shell."

"I ask again, what happened?"

"The king marked and claimed me. I'm whole once again, and now I belong to the king as I once did to the carue."

"So, now the king can take you over."

"He could, but he won't because he believes I'll function better outside direct control."

"She's right, Igor," said Ella, as she lightly gripped his arm. "You know that Harald has marked and claimed all the household staff as well as the grounds keepers. He leaves them free to do their jobs because he knows they will do their best for him, always.

"Igor, what Larise did before was the carue's desires for safety from us, under its control. It couldn't depend on her without that.

Remember how she always worked with us when not under direct control.

"Now, under Harald's mark, she will always have free will. He won't try to control her; he doesn't have to. He knows she's completely devoted to him and his people now."

"So now we're supposed to trust her?"

"Yes," replied Ella.

"I will, completely," grinned Gudrun. "Harald's marked her, she's one of us now, body and soul."

Igor looked at the two vampires for a moment then nodded. "I believe you both, and I will trust that. Ronni?"

"If Ella and Gudrun are good with it, so am I. I've got no grudge here."

"Thank you for that, Lady Hawk. I know what I did, and I'll make it up to you, I swear I will."

"That wasn't you, it was the carue, but if you insist, you can start now."

"Tell me what you need," replied Larise.

"I need you and Bran to make peace," replied Rhonda.

"No," said Branimir, backing away.

"Yes," said Igor, as he grabbed his friend's arm and propelled him toward the bed where Larise sat, her hands folded in her lap. "Bran, you know that was the carue, as do I. You need to make peace with her and so do I. As your alpha, I'm ordering you to go first. Talk to each other. The rest of us are going to the bar for some food."

With that, he rose and led the others out the door, leaving Branimir alone with Larise. "Do you think it safe to put them together like that so soon?" asked Rhonda, as she linked her arm through Igor's.

"No, it isn't, but his wolf is still called to her, I can feel that. They need to get this settled, and I need time to absorb the fact that the king claimed her and now she bears his mark. I need to fully understand and believe what that means so I can instinctively trust in it.

"I need food, I need to dance with my beautiful Lady Hawk, then I need ten hours sleep. After that I'm going to figure out how to track down that damned vampire."

Branimir watched the door close then turned to Larise who hadn't moved from her place on the bed, she was looking down at her shoes. Finally, she couldn't take the silence any longer. "Bran, I see you retained your place in your pack. I'm relieved to know that. It broke my heart to see you destroyed like that."

"You have a heart?"

"Not when the carue controlled me, no, but otherwise, yes. Bran, you said you loved me and I betrayed you. That's partly true, but not the way you think. I'm not wolf, I'm human, and I first arrived with a lot of baggage, trust issues. You came on pretty strong, and that scared me."

"Scared you? Why? How? I made no ..."

"No, no you didn't, Bran. It scared me because I liked it too much. Do you understand? I was completely messed up, and I guess I was expecting you to run games on me like all other men did. I didn't know about werewolves, didn't know how you operate, what makes you tick.

"Yes, I liked your attention, more than I let you know, and it broke me when you threw me against that tree and told me what I'd done. Once you killed the carue I was emptied out, a shell. I remember how much I'd liked being with you, but had no attachment to it. It was all like everything had happened to someone else, a stranger."

"And now?"

She looked up at last, her eyes glistening. "Now I remember the times you complimented me and were sincere, the times you held me gently, and I miss them terribly. I know that, after what all happened, you don't want me near. I'll do my best to stay out of your way."

Branimir sighed deeply and sat beside her. "You still don't know shit about wolves."

"Bran?"

"Wolves mate for life, Larise. Yes, I hated you, released you, but that was from my head. My wolf heart still cried out for you, and I've mourned the loss of you every moment since then. I will for the rest of my life."

"Bran, what are you saying here? Are you saying you want to try again?"

"Da. May the gods help me and curse me for a weak fool, but, yes, I'm still drawn to you."

"But you said you released me, doesn't that mean ...?"

"It means that I would live my life without you, never speak your name aloud. I would mate, have pups, and do my best to make life beautiful for whatever woman would have me, but my heart would ever be yours. That's the way of the wolf, our kind of wolf."

"Bran, I'm all brand new. The king remade me, gave me back the person I was before the carue took me, before the other troubles. He made me the person I could have been. I want to live up to that. I won't push, but do you think you can you set aside your anger and sorrow, get to know me as the person I am now."

"Da, on one condition. You have to take me to the bar and feed me. We've been chasing that damned vampire for days without food or rest. So, I ask you, are you the kind of woman who'd buy a guy a meal?"

"Yes, but only if he was a special guy, a forgiving guy, a gentle loving guy who can turn into a big bad wolf." She rose and pulled him to his feet. "Come on, big guy, let's go get some meat into you." She took his arm and led him to the bar where the music was loud, and the smell of food was in the air.

They entered to see Igor slow dancing with Rhonda, Ella and Gudrun returning through the back door, and the server setting a gigantic platter of food on the table where Kylie sat waiting. "So, did you two kiss and make up?" she asked, as Bran and Larise sat down and he dug into the chicken wings with a will.

"Not quite," replied Larise, "but I think we might get there someday. How about you, Kylie? Will you give me a chance?"

"Sure. King Harald marked you, you're safe now."

"I've had my shots?"

"Yeah, that," grinned Kylie. "Hey, sport, are you planning to save any of that for the rest of us?"

"No," Bran muttered around the bones of a chicken wing. She just grinned, then kissed Ella's cheek as the vampires joined them.

Igor and Rhonda sat with them and then it became a scramble for the food. "Stop it, both of you," admonished Rhonda, as she slapped at Igor and Branimir. "You're acting like a couple of hungry dogs. Settle down and I'll order more wings." She raised her arm and the girl hurried over.

Gathering up the empty baskets she winked at Gudrun. "The boys are hungry tonight."

"They've been getting lots of exercise lately," replied Gudrun with a sly grin.

"I don't even want to know," laughed the girl, as she hurried away, soon to return with more chicken wings. "So, how'd that stain work out?"

"Everything's all cleaned up," replied Gudrun.

"Good to know." She gave Gudrun a knowing nod of approval and scurried away.

Ella sighed and leaned back in her chair. She was well sated and ready for some rest. "When you guys are finished eating the legs off the table, get some sleep. That's where I'm going right now."

"First we should take a look around, you know, just in case a certain something has doubled back," said Gudrun.

"Relax, guys," said Rhonda. "I'll do it. You folks get some sleep."

"Little sister, don't you ever tire?" asked Gudrun, as she rose to her feet.

"Nope," grinned Rhonda. "Okay, I'll fess up, I can rest on the fly, as it were."

"You're joking."

"Nope."

"That's cheating."

"You're just jealous."

"Damn right I am. I'm going now, I have to take Mother back to her room."

"I'll help you," grinned Kylie.

"If I hear one old joke out of either of you," threatened Ella, "there'll be trouble and you'll both be in it." She rolled her eyes as they each took her arm and escorted her from the bar.

"They've got the right idea," said Igor. "Come on, let's get some rest." He dropped a huge tip on the table then they left, heading back towards the motel. "So, you two okay?"

"We're working on it," replied Bran. Igor nodded, that was good enough for him.

Larise had already checked into a new room. As she unlocked the door, Bran stepped in behind her. She turned and looked at him with mischief in her eyes. "Still bodyguarding me?"

"Do you mind?"

"No, I like the idea. You get the bed, you're beat, I'm not. I'll take the chair." For an answer he morphed into the wolf and curled up in the chair. "All right, if that's the way you want it. No peeking while I get undressed."

He sighed deeply and rested his chin on the arm of the chair. He was asleep before she got her shirt off. Larise gazed at the wolf for a long time. "I wonder," she thought, "will he ever truly forgive me, or is this just his instinct taking over. Doesn't matter, I guess. At least I've got a chance."

The next morning, Larise awakened to the sun shining through the window. She tried to stretch but there was something heavy on the bed.

She opened her eyes to see the wolf lying there, gazing at her with sad eyes. Larise beamed him her best smile and tousled her hair. "Good morning, Bran, did you sleep with me all night or is this your way of waking me up in the morning?"

He didn't move so she slowly extended her hand toward him, reaching to scratch behind his ears. He licked her hand once then rose and hopped off the bed, morphed into the man, and pulled on his clothes. "We should hurry and get some breakfast; Igor will be in a rush."

"Bran? What is it? Bran, are we okay?"

He turned those sad eyes on her and gently cupped her cheek in a huge hand. "Da, we're good, Larise."

"Are you sure?"

"I'm sure. I'm just shaking off an old dream. I need coffee."

"Plus eggs, ham, bacon, and sausage?"

That brought a smile to his face. "Da, all of that. Let's go."

The café was only open until noon, but it opened early and served a hearty breakfast. As they stepped through the door they saw the others already there. Igor raised his arm and pointed at them. The woman behind the counter grinned and brought two huge platters of food to the table.

"So, Bran, everything okay?"

"Da."

"Bullshit, as Eric would say. I need you to focus on the hunt."

"I will," he replied around a mouthful of ham. He swallowed then spoke again. "The small one will have been hungry when she reached the highway. She was newly revived and had fought the great mother, barely escaping with her life. She wouldn't have gone far before losing control and killing whoever picked her up. We need to hunt along that road until we find where she killed and fed, then we can track her again."

"That was my thought," agreed Igor. "Eat lots, it could be days before we find her."

"Listen, guys," said Rhonda, "it'll be a lot faster if I do it. You stay with the cars, drive slow, keeping me in sight. I'll fly the roadside until I find a car or something, some possible sign of her, and then you can check it out. Sooner or later you'll catch her scent."

"Works for me," said Igor. "Kylie and Larise stay here and work the electronics. You might pick up something to give us a clue to where she's gone."

"Your place or mine?" asked Larise, as she turned to Kylie.

"Our room, I'm already set up there. I'll work the internet while you monitor the TV news channels and police radio."

"We have a plan," smiled Larise.

WHILE THE HUNTERS SET out along the highway, an older woman sat guarding the sleep of the small child, her mind in turmoil. She'd hadn't been aware they'd had a grandchild, she'd born no children, but the girl had come to the cabin door and called her Grandma. What happened after that was fuzzy in her mind.

She remembered screaming, but couldn't remember why. She gazed at the body of the man on the floor. She knew him, they'd been married for many years. The sight made her heart ache, but the sound of the child stirring in her sleep commanded her attention. She tucked the girl back in then picked up the sewing. The doll was in bad shape and Mistress had said to fix it.

The Hunt Goes On

The vampire king sat patiently waiting for the queen to surface from her trance. Slowly she shook it off and sighed deeply. "Sally, my love?"

"She's killed again, Harald. Worse, she's claimed a woman to serve her. The poor soul is trying to fix the child's doll with her dead husband on the floor beside her. Harald, any illusions I had about rehabilitating this beast are gone. The child enjoys the cruelty of the kill. They have to make an end of her."

"Sally, what else is distressing you? Sweet woman, I can feel your anguish from here."

"Harald, when they kill the vampire that poor woman will find herself bereft and alone with the body of her dead husband. It would have been kinder if the vampire had killed her outright."

"Ella will have to put a compulsion on her, explain it all in a way everyone can accept."

"Harald, that will leave her like Larise was, barely alive, unable to care for herself, or even willing to."

"I understand, my sweet, I do, but what other option do we have? Sally, I can't mark every lost ..."

"I know, I know," she replied, gently placing her fingers on his lips. "I know, my love, but if I can devise something, find a use for her skills, something that would be a true benefit to us ..."

"All right, sweet Sally," chuckled Harald, as he lightly kissed her fingers then pulled her into his arms. "If there is a true benefit to bringing this woman here, we'll do it, but ..."

"I know, sweetheart, it has to be a real benefit for the Lair, for the people."

THE HUNTERS SET OUT, with the Lady Hawk flying high overhead. She returned to where they'd lost the trail before, then turned south along the highway, making long looping circles, always swinging back to overlap, making certain she missed nothing.

The day wore on and their slow progress attracted the attention of both impatient motorists and the local police. Each time they were stopped Igor flashed his badge and sent them on their way. Darkness was falling when the hawk began to make a tight circle to the left just off the highway.

A short ride on a dirt road led them to an abandoned car with a dead body beside it. The man had been drained of blood. The scent was clear, the shapeshifters transformed, and the wolves were on her trail once again. Gudrun grinned as she watched the tigress follow the dire wolves into the trees. She folded up their clothes then locked up the car and followed them.

When it became too dark to see they stopped to rest for the night but were on the go at the first hint of light. Before noon they found the lonely cabin with the dead man inside, the vampire was nowhere to be found.

Branimir was the first to find the trail, and with a yap to call the others, he set out once again. The day was late when they found the crying woman. She was battered, scratched, and her clothes were torn. "She left me behind," sobbed the woman. "Please help me. Please leave her alone and help me."

"She's a decoy," said Gudrun, as she caught up. "Get the vampire's scent, find her, she'll be moving faster now." Igor and Branimir were off into the trees once again with Ella close behind.

Gudrun turned to the woman and sighed. *"Listen to me. You got lost in the forest. Go home now. Your husband had an accident with a chainsaw. Go to him and bury the body. You will forget all about seeing me or the other animals. Go."*

Without another word the woman turned back toward the cabin where the body of her husband was now lying beside the woodpile, the chainsaw right beside him. Gudrun then set out after the hunting wolves.

Once again they stopped when it became too dark to see. The hawk dropped easily down to morph into the woman. She cuddled close to Igor who transformed to take her in his arms. "We're getting closer now, sweet Ronni," he sighed. "She's no longer on her home turf, doesn't know where the hiding places are, and so she runs. We're closing in. Soon we'll make an end of her and go back to finish up the job then go home."

"Finish up the job?" asked Gudrun.

"Miss Gudrun, there were several wrong animals at that ghost town, animals tainted by the carue, plus there was a second carue. I want to go back and comb the area all around that town, make certain there are no more, and dispose of any we do find. I plan to make certain the area is clear before I tell the king the job is finished."

"That's good thinking, little brother," she smiled, as she patted his shoulder.

They settled down for the night but were on the move before first light. By the end of day they still hadn't caught up to their quarry. Darkness was falling, but this time Igor wouldn't stop. He and Branimir continued to follow the scent and the hawk remained vigilant overhead. They pushed on, finding dead animals on the trail. The vampire was getting tired, hungry, and desperate. Dawn was breaking when they burst from the trees and found themselves back on the highway. This time she'd gone north.

The hawk spiraled down and morphed into the woman. "Looks like she's trying to get back to her home turf. You guys wait here, I'll go for the car." Gudrun tossed the keys into the air and the hawk caught them in her talons. With a piercing cry she disappeared into the morning sky.

When Rhonda arrived with the car they swiftly dressed, burned a U-turn, and headed back toward Tanner's Ridge. Gudrun called Kylie while Rhonda drove, so she and Larise had food waiting when they arrived.

"Okay, what's our next move?" asked Larise.

"We know she headed back this way," said Igor. "We can assume she'll return to her old lair. We got too close to her, and she retreated to familiar ground. The problem is, she knows the caves too well. We'll have the devil's own time trying to catch her."

"You need bait," said Larise.

"Bait?"

"Bait. She'll be hungry, frightened, but she has to feed, and you've been pushing her hard, she needs to feed and rest. We need to bait her out."

"What are you suggesting here, Larise?"

"You guys go wolf and tiger, head into her territory, but give her a bit of space. I'll go in alone. She'll recognize me as the carue's and she'll come for me."

"No," said Branimir. "No, Larise, it's too dangerous."

"We have no other choice and you know it. Bran, I'll go in heavy, guns and ammo. Lady Hawk can keep me in sight and signal you when I lure her out."

"No, Larise."

"Yes, Bran, I have to do this. I owe you all this. Trust me, I'm a survivor, I can do this."

Ella stepped forward and put her arm around the girl's shoulders. "We'll be near at all times."

"All right," said Igor. "We've got some daylight left, let's go." They gave it full effort, but darkness fell and no sign of the vampire. They retreated to their motel for rest and a meal at the bar.

THE SMALL VAMPIRE HUDDLED in her old cave, she was angry, and yet fearful. She hugged the newly repaired doll to her chest. "It's not fair, Maggie. They chased us everywhere. They found us and the new mother we made. We had to come back, Maggie, we had to. Those nasty people want to hurt us. They'd take you away like the bad man did long ago.

"We can't stay here, either, Maggie. The scent is old, but they were here, in our home. We'll move to a new cave until they get tired and go away. We'll pick a small one that they can't get into. We'll make sure it has a back door too. We'll be extra careful, Maggie, until they get tired and go away.

"Wish I wasn't so hungry though, and I know you're hungry too. Let's go see if we can find a deer or something. We'll avoid humans until those bad people go away, then we'll make a new carue. This time the carue will be ours, not his, and it'll help us." She continued to talk to and sooth her doll through much of the night. By morning she'd moved to a much smaller cave but hadn't managed to feed herself.

NEXT MORNING THEY SET out again. Larise started at the ghost town and slowly worked her way towards the vampire's lair. By noon she'd reached it, but the beast wasn't there. A careful study of the ground told Larise she'd been there but was gone. Dammit anyway.

"All right," muttered Larise, "where would she go? To a smaller cave. We've been in her lair and our scent would still be there. That's no longer safe, so she'd look for a smaller cave, one close to other caves and one with a second entrance. Shit, this could take some time."

Larise checked her weapons, then left the cave mouth for another. From the corner of her eye she saw the movement of a dark body as the wolf moved silently through the dense undergrowth. The second wolf and the tigress would be close, she knew.

By the end of day there was still no sign of the vampire, and so they retreated to the motel once again.

LARISE DIDN'T SEE THE hidden killer, hidden by the mouth of the small cave, but she saw Larise, and her companions.

"I know Maggie, I know, it's the carue's woman, but the others are following too close to her. I think she might be helping them. Maybe our new carue can take control of her like the old one did.

"Yes, I know you're hungry, I am too, so hungry, but we have to wait and be careful. I've called to the new one, Maggie. She should be here tomorrow then we can eat her. We'll be okay then, we just have to wait one more day.

"THIS ISN'T WORKING," grumbled Igor.

"It's not working because you guys are staying too close," sighed Larise. "She can scent you as easily as you can scent her. She's frightened, and wary, especially of Ella. She attacked the tigress and got a fast lesson in how bad an idea that was. Her instincts are as sharp as yours, and she's scared.

"Guys, we need her to believe I'm alone. You've got to give her more space."

"We dare not, Larise," said Ella. "If she attacks you, your time for rescue is quite finite."

"Then it won't work and we're back where we started. People, do this, give me more space. She'll take the bait; I know she will."

"She's right," said Gudrun. "I saw no signs of her feeding, and that's not something she tries to hide. If we back off a bit she'll come, but I do suggest body armor and something thick to protect your neck, Larise. You'll have to survive several seconds until one of us can get there.

"Are you certain you can do this. Perhaps I should be the bait."

"That won't work, Gudrun," said Larise. "As I understand it, she'll know you're a vampire. She'll keep her distance from you."

"Yeah," sighed Gudrun, "she will."

"All right," said Igor. "Let's try again tomorrow, but you be careful, Larise."

"I will, I promise."

Terror's End

"There she is again, Maggie, alone this time. It's risky, but we're so hungry. I can't stand it, Maggie, I can't. We have to eat. I have to kill something and she's right there. Our other one still isn't here, so we'll eat this one then we'll eat the other one when it gets here. That'll be good, won't it, Maggie. All those new bones to play with. You wait right here, Maggie. I won't be long."

With that, the small vampire slipped out of her hiding place and began to stalk the lone woman on the street of the deserted town.

MORNING CAME AND ONCE again Larise was scouting around the ghost town. This time she appeared to be alone. She was staying out in the open more to give her companions a clear path should they need it. Not only was she wearing body armor, but she'd cut the top off a cowboy boot to make a thick leather choker to protect her neck. By midafternoon they'd still had no success, and then they heard the car approaching.

Thinking it might be Kylie, Ella stepped out into the road just before the town became visible. As soon as the driver spotted her the car sped up and shot past. It was the woman from the cabin who'd tried to slow them down before. Ella started to give chase, but Gudrun stopped her.

"Let her go, Mother, she might lead us to her master." Ella nodded then shimmered back into the tigress. They both followed the car, staying just out of sight in the trees.

The car drove right up to lone figure on the street and the woman got out, a shotgun in her hands. Before she could shoot or make a threat, Larise moved, and the shotgun was gone from the woman's hands. Larise tossed it aside.

"Please," begged the woman. "you have to go away and leave her alone."

"No."

"But you have to. Just go away and she won't hurt me. Please, just go."

Before Larise could respond she heard the warning cry of the hawk, and a wolf broke from cover, racing toward her. Instinctively she ducked and rolled away; that saved her life. The blow meant for her killed the other woman.

The vampire turned and leaped back at Larise, but was met by a hail of gunfire from her intended victim. However, her speed hurled her wounded body into Larise, knocking them both to the ground. Before she could sink her fangs into her victim, the jaws of the wolf clamped down hard and she was ripped away from Larise.

The vampire shook off the wolf, then looked down at her bleeding chest. She looked up again as the tigress slammed into her, knocking her to the ground. Mighty jaws bit hard and the head was ripped away from the body. The vampire lay dead on the ground at last.

"Larise, are you all right?" asked Branimir.

"I'll have a few bruises, but the sight of a handsome guy, buck naked, offering to help me up is making the pain go away."

He chuckled as he helped her to her feet. "She's fine, Igor."

"Good to know," he grinned, as the hawk changed in mid-flight to land in his arms. "The other woman is dead?"

"She is," said Gudrun, as she scooped up the vampire's head and dropped it into a plastic bag.

"Then we're down to the clean-up," sighed Igor. Let's get those bodies out of sight, then call it a day. "I'll report to the king then we can get some rest. Tomorrow I have to think of something to do with all the corpses lying around, then we sweep the area to make sure there are no more carue or disturbed animals. With luck we'll be home in a few days."

"You and Bran sweep the area for pests," said Gudrun. "I'll take care of the bodies for you."

"Miss Gudrun?"

"I'll stack them with the bones in the vampire's cave then have Eric bring some explosives. We'll seal up the evidence inside. Tonight, I'll take the head to the animal crematorium and make damn sure that little bugger can't come back."

"Works for me," said Igor. "Let's go."

THEY GATHERED AT THE motel to bring Kylie up to speed, and get her take on the cover story she was working on. After, as they retired for the night, Bran noticed Larise staring out the window, thoughtfully.

"Larise, you okay?"

"Huh? Oh, yeah, I'm all good. I was just thinking about the vampire."

"Oh?"

"Yeah, did you see that rag doll she had in her pocket?"

"Ah-huh. So?"

"So, she was just a kid, Bran. She couldn't have been more than ten years old when that happened to her, her life stripped away before she had a chance, turned into a monster, and spending the next sixty years trying to figure it out and live with it. The others had Ella to help them, teach them, you guys had Ella and the king to save you, help you, teach you. She had nobody."

"You feel sorry for the vampire?"

"I do, sort of. I know what it's like to have someone, something, take you over and ruin your life. I was lucky, the king saved me, gave me a second chance, you all did. That kid had nothing, no chance at all."

"Yeah, I guess. Larise, you can't ..."

"I know, big guy, I know. No compassion for the enemy under battle conditions, that gets you killed in a hurry. By the way, thanks for ripping her off me. Damn, I put a full clip into her and it barely slowed her down."

"She was tough all right. She threw me off easy as you please."

"Yeah." Larise sighed. "I'm feeling a bit weird tonight. Can we cuddle in that big chair and watch some mindless TV for a while?" He didn't answer so she turned away and pulled off her shirt. "Okay, I get it. Too soon. I'll just crawl into bed and ..."

"Larise."

"Yeah?"

"If you're cold you can have wolf cuddles."

"Actually, I'd rather have Bran's arms around me, if you can do that."

"Da, I can do that, and I want to. Come on, snuggle in here with me and show me how to use this damn remote." With a shy smile she came and cuddled into his arms, resting her head on his shoulder.

"You scared me today," he whispered.

"Yeah?"

"Yeah, you took an awful chance."

"My reflexes are pretty good, so I figured I could last until somebody got there. I heard Ronni scream and I ducked. Man, that thing was fast. I pumped her full of lead and she still put me down. Thanks for tearing her off me."

"You scared me," he repeated and tightened his arms around her. She nodded and cuddled closer.

"HARALD HERE."

"Sire, it's Igor."

"Sally tells me you've had some success at last."

"Yes, we finally managed to make an end of the other vampire."

"She gave you hard run, Igor. Don't let it get to you, we vampires are hard to kill."

"Da, and harder to catch."

The king chuckled at that. "So, are you all done out there?"

"I believe we are, Sire, but I want to make sure. That carue made a lot of un-natural animals, and the vampire made a few too. I want to let Kylie finish up with the official story, and while she does that I want to make a full sweep of the area, clean out any unusual things that shouldn't be here."

"Need any help?"

"Miss Gudrun wants Eric with a bag full of explosives. There are a number of human bodies as well as a cave nearly full of bones collected by the vampire. She wants to pile the bodies in the cave then collapse it like you did in Scotland when you rescued us."

"Eric's right here, Igor. Just a minute." Igor heard the king talking to Eric then he was back on the line. "He's on his way, Igor. He'll be there by morning. Do you need anything else?"

"I hope not, Sire. This whole thing almost got away from us."

"It all too often does," chuckled the king. "Remember when you went to Boone with Terry. Things can get away from the best of us. The key is to keep your head until you see the path through. So, tell me, how did Larise do?"

"She did great, Sire. She was the key to the final success."

"She insisted on being the bait to lure the vampire out of hiding?"

"Da, she did. Crazy woman."

"So, do we keep her or send her back to the government."

Igor chuckled at that. "I think we have to keep her. I doubt Bran will let her go."

"Good to know," chuckled Harald. "Stay in touch, Igor."

"Everything okay with the king?" asked Rhonda.

"A-okay, sweet Ronni," replied Igor, as he stripped off and crawled into bed beside her.

"Good, now you can pay attention to your wife for a change."

"For a change? That's hardly fair, I've been tracking a vampire, running a crew, directing a ..."

"Shut up and kiss me like you mean it, silly wolf."

Igor chuckled and pulled her close.

THE NEXT MORNING THEY went for breakfast to find Eric already there. He grinned at Gudrun and tapped his watch. She shook a threatening finger at him then went for coffee. Once breakfast was finished, they left for the ghost town to finish up the job. They found the new sheriff and his deputy, plus another man already there.

"Morning, Agent Wolf."

"Good morning, Sheriff, is it? Enjoying the promotion?"

"Up until right now, I was. Hank here decided to hunt this area today. Man's a damn fool, folks haven't hunted in this area for years. Anybody who tried never returned. Now, Hank here, he came blasting into my office, interrupting my morning coffee, and babbling about dead bodies all over the place.

"As the sheriff, I'm obliged to check out these sorts of things, and sure enough, old Hank was right, dead bodies everywhere. Any idea what the hell happened here, and where's that little girl's head?"

Igor sighed deeply and looked away toward the morning sun shining on the snowcapped mountains. "Do you really want to know, Sheriff?"

He looked back, and the man was studying him. "You know, Agent Wolf, I'm not so sure I do, but, the job and all ..."

"All right, Sheriff, here's what I can share with you. We're just finishing up here. The thing that was haunting this place, killing all those people, is now dead. It took us a while to corner it and finish it off, but we managed it. I can't tell you what it was because I don't actually know. The carcass is already on its way to a government lab.

"Back during the cold war, before either of us were born, the government experimented with things better left alone. Some of it got away from them and some things are still on the loose. That's what our team does, we find those things and make them disappear. Now, if you ever repeat any of that somebody will come and make you disappear."

"I believe you, Agent. So, you're actually a clean-up crew?"

"Yes, we are. I have to tell you; this one was a tough case. I believe we're almost done here, but I want to cruise the area one more time to make sure we got it all. That thing has been here a long time."

"So, how do I write this up?"

"Dangerous volcanic gasses," replied Igor, "very corrosive, eats away the bodies. People should avoid the area. This woman is Agent West, she'll fill you in."

Ella stepped closer then spoke in that voice from an alien hell. *"Obey me. You will believe what Agent Wolf has told you, but you will never speak of it. You, hunter, you found nothing here, just the sheriff, you talked, then you went away. You will never hunt this area again.*

"Sheriff, you will bury this case deep and never speak of it. If anyone asks, the Feds took the case and handled it themselves. You know nothing more about it. Warn people about the dangerous gasses, warn them away. Go now."

As soon as she finished speaking all three men got in their vehicles and drove away. Igor sighed and turned back to the scene. Eric and Gudrun were already carrying bodies into the forest. Suddenly the hawk called a warning and swooped towards them.

She morphed into the woman as she touched the ground. "Transform, incoming carue," she shouted, then leaped skyward once again.

"Crap," muttered Igor, as he transformed to the dire wolf. Branimir and Ella had changed as well. Gudrun signaled Eric to get back with Larise, then she put herself between them and whatever was crashing through the trees towards them. They soon saw what it was.

Something huge stumbled out of the undergrowth and into the open space of the ghost town. It looked to be half man and half huge bear. It was roaring in pain and confusion as it stumbled forward.

This creature obviously had no idea what it was or what had happened to it. It was hurting, confused, and desperately hungry for blood. Spotting the animals, it made a shambling charge, but the tigress met it halfway. The mighty beast fought with a desperate fury, but it was no match for the saber-tooth.

A blow from the big cat sent it sprawling, but it rose and swung a clawed hand at the tigress. It knocked her back, bleeding, but that was all. Its next blow missed, but the cat didn't. Great claws raked down the creature's side, then another knocked it flat.

The cat instantly leaped on it, powerful front paws and foot long fangs held it firmly while mighty back claws raked and raked at the creature's exposed belly. Within moments it lay dead, but the others held back.

The tigress was still spoiling for a fight. She continued to roar her challenge as she paced about, battering at the fallen carue. Finally she stopped and transformed back into the woman. With a saucy grin, Gudrun passed Ella her clothes.

"Dear, sweet, baby Jesus," breathed Larise, as Ella got dressed. "I thought you were scary before."

"You still haven't seen anything," grinned Gudrun. "I've seen her take on several vampires at once. None survived. What the hell ever made Mobutu think he could take her, I'll never know.

"Come on, Eric, let's get these last two bodies into that cave and drop that mountain down on it."

"I'll help you," said Ella. "Igor, you and Bran go ahead and sweep the area. It's time to clean up this mess and go home."

The wolf gave her a friendly nudge then set out, his companion close behind. Larise swept up Eric's pack and followed him into the trees. They stowed the bodies, then Eric set the charges and they pulled back. The explosion had the desired effect, the cave was completely collapsed.

They returned to the car to find Rhonda waiting for them. "Go on back folks. I know Igor well. He'll be a day or two before he's satisfied the area is clear. I'll stay with the boys; you guys go back and get some rest."

"Perhaps I should stay, just in case," said Ella.

"It's all right, Ella, go back and get a meal, snuggle with your girl. There's nothing else anywhere near here. Believe me, I've been looking."

"Then why ...?"

"Igor, you know what he's like. Yes, he trusts my vision, but he'll check for scent anyway, just to be sure."

"And Bran will stay with him," said Larise.

"Igor's the alpha, where he goes, so will his pack. Get used to it, girl. If you're planning to bond with Branimir, you'd better get used to it."

Larise chuckled at that. "Yeah, I guess it's like when I used to get called out at all hours."

"Very much the same, I'm sure. Go on guys, go get some rest, maybe pack up some of our stuff and take a load back to the plane. Maybe one of you can bring the other car for us tomorrow. They should be finished by then."

TWO DAYS LATER, THE wolves came out of the forest and trotted over to the waiting car. Larise grinned as she handed them their clothes.

The hawk came swooping in, did a backward flip as she morphed into Rhonda who landed easily on her feet and reached for her dress and shoes.

"Show off," grinned Igor.

"You like it," she replied with a grin of her own. "Is everything else all set, Larise?"

"Yep, Kylie finished up the reports, gave me the sheriff's copies and sent the rest on to Director Bridger. Ella and Gudrun have everything else all packed up and loaded on the plane. We just have to turn in the car and hop on board."

"Any chance we could stop for breakfast?" asked Branimir.

"Sure, big guy, I'll buy you breakfast. We have to drop off the reports for the sheriff, then we can hit that café across the street. That work for you?"

"What are we waiting for?" he asked, as he climbed into the passenger's seat. Larise grinned as she drove down the mountain to the sheriff's office.

They dropped off the paperwork, then went to the café. Bran saw the old fellow sitting quietly by the chess board. "Order me something," he said, as he patted Larise on the shoulder. He went to the booth and swiftly set up the pieces. "Quick one?"

"Sure," replied the old man, as he made a move which Bran instantly countered. "You have any luck? I see you're still breathing."

Bran made another move then nodded. "It's dead."

The old man countered the move. "It?"

"Them," replied Bran.

"All?"

"All, every damn one of them."

The old man's hand shook as he made the next move. "That's a good thing," he said at last. "Why bother telling me?"

"Because you, of all people, deserved to know. Damn, you got me again." Grinning, he stood and shook the old man's hand. "Thanks for the game."

"Anytime, son," replied the old man. "Any time at all."

Larise turned back to the table, she'd been watching Bran and the old man. "That boy's got class."

"Yep, he's a keeper all right," smiled Rhonda.

"Yeah, I just hope I can."

"Work on it."

"I am."

Just then Bran returned to the table and sat. There was a platter of food waiting for him, bacon, eggs, ham, and sausage. He grinned and looked at Larise. "I thought you might be hungry," she smiled.

"Hungry as a wolf," he said, as he tucked in.

Final Assessment

They arrived back at the castle to find Elaine and Charles waiting for them. "You folks go on; the king's in the great hall. We'll take care of the bags for you," said Charles.

"Thank you, Charles," replied Ella, as she stepped away from the plane.

Branimir started to follow, but Elaine placed her hand on his chest to stop him. He gazed into her eyes and she arched an eyebrow at him then glanced at Larise. "It's a work in progress," he said softly.

"Work harder," she replied.

"Elaine?"

"This is still hurting," she said as she patted his chest over his heart, "and so is hers. Heal each other, you know you can and so you must. Stop wasting time."

"Was that an order?" he asked, a grin playing at his lips.

"Yes it was," she replied, a twinkle in her eye, "and if you ever want any more of those treats ..."

"Understood, my sister," he smiled, as he kissed the top of her head.

He turned to see Larise gazing at him, the pleading clear in her eyes. Bran let go of his resistance and let his wolf choose for him. He reached for Larise and tucked her under his arm. "Come, Larise, the alpha female has spoken and we have no choice."

"Don't want one," she replied, as she stepped closer and put her arm around his waist.

"No, me neither. Let's go, we have to report in." Together, and in perfect step, they followed the others to the great hall.

The king was there with Terry and Queen Sally when they arrived. "Sit, my friends, sit," smiled the king. "So, it's done, finished?"

"I believe so, Sire," replied Igor, "as much as can be without stationing people there permanently."

"Igor?"

"Sire, we killed one vampire and three carue, as well as a dozen or more tainted animals, plus a number of humans. Bran and I scouted the area thoroughly for scent, and Ronni checked from above for movement. For the moment it's clear, however, we have reservations. I will ask Miss Ella to explain."

"Mother?"

"It's a complete mess, Harald. As best I can understand from what we learned and what we saw, Mobutu paid that town a visit many years ago. You know what he was like, and this was typical of things he did.

"As I see it, he made several vampires and carue, then set them loose on the town. Once the slaughter was finished he would have killed all his creations as was his habit, but I believe several managed to escape him.

"If that little one was as hard to catch in those days as she was when we hunted her, she would have driven him to madness, giving other of his creations time to put distance between them. We have no idea at all what or how many managed to survive, or where they might appear in the future."

"Well that's a bit disturbing, but nothing we can do about it now; we don't have the people to make a prolonged hunt of that magnitude. For now we'll call this one a win, case closed. Well done, Igor."

"Thank you, Sire."

"Tell me, how did Larise perform when she returned to you?"

"She was so different, Sire, a real asset to us."

The king leaned his elbows on the table. "Yes, Larise, about setting yourself out as bait for a vampire. Don't do it again."

The poor woman looked seriously distressed. "Sire, I'm ..."

"Relax, girl, I'm just teasing you. Igor, what's the verdict? Do we keep her or send her back to the government?"

"Keep her, Sire, or I'll be stuck with a sulky, brooding wolf for a hundred years." This brought a round of chuckles.

"What say you, Larise," asked the king. "Will you remain with us?"

"I'd truly like to, Sire. I'm enjoying having a personal bodyguard."

"What say you, Branimir, are you ready for a long-term job as a bodyguard?"

"I think I can handle it, Sire," he grinned. "Now that you've got her house-broken the job's not as dangerous as it was."

Larise spun around to see the teasing grin on his face and her heart sang. "You think so, buddy? Well, you ain't seen nothing yet. You just wait until I get you alone."

"Be still my heart."

"All right," sighed the king. "Take it outside, you two." He smiled as Bran took Larise by the hand and led her out of the room. "Terry, is her staying here going to be a problem for the director?"

"Not really, Sire. It was Compton who put her in the job. He chose her for her assets, not her abilities, if you get what I mean."

"I do indeed."

"Egan sent her out west on a wild goose chase hoping to be rid of her for a while. He'll be more than happy to let her go so he can put someone else in her job, someone more capable."

"He'll have a damned hard time finding one," said Gudrun.

"She's really that good?" asked Terry.

"Larise faced a vampire on full attack mode and survived long enough for Ella to reach them. There's not many humans who could do that."

"Awesome," grinned Terry. "I'll call Egan and give him the bad news; this'll be fun."

Outside the castle, beneath a huge oak tree, Branimir pulled Larise close and kissed her. "The wolf mates for life," he whispered as their lips slowly parted.

"Good, that means you won't try to get away from me. Wouldn't do you any good to try, I'm a trained agent, after all. Yes, my big bad wolf, I know it's a forever deal, I like it this way. Now kiss me like you mean it."

He did, and it was far more gentle and tender than she expected. This man was so very different from any other she had known. Cuddled into his arms, Larise knew she'd found her safe place at last.

The End

Author's note: Our friends can enjoy a rest for a while, but there's something amiss on the western wind. Let's take a closer look. Just turn the page and ...

Race the Wind

By
Prudence MacLeod
(second edition)

Premonition

The queen of the vampires awakened with a start, breathing deeply as she tried to shake off the spell of the vision. "Sally, my beloved, what is it?" Concerned, the king took her gently into his arms. "Hush now, I've got you, you're safe. Tell me what you saw."

She snuggled against him, retreating into the protection of his arms. "I saw a time of danger, Harald, danger of discovery. Somehow, a horse is at the center of it, but it's Igor and Rhonda who are the key."

"Igor and Rhonda?"

"Yes, if they can't hold true to each other, all will be lost. If they can, we have a solid chance, but it's the horse that will make or break it."

"So what do we do?"

"Nothing, Harald, my love. There's nothing we can do. It's going to be up to the Hawk and the Wolf; our future lies in their hands, their ability to function, the strength of their love for each other. This will be their greatest test, and all our fates hang in the balance.

"Harald, we can't let them know. We can't tell a single soul until it's over. We just have to believe in them and trust them to prove true to each other."

He hugged her shoulders gently then sighed. "Well, both hawks and wolves mate for life, that much is in our favor. Is there nothing at all we can do?"

"We can help them if they ask, no more. Harald, you poor man, it must be torture being married to a psychic."

With a chuckle, he hugged her again. "Actually, I quite like it, and being forewarned before danger arrives is never a bad thing. Do you know what the danger is?"

"Exposure to the public."

He sighed again. "Damn."

Wild Horses

"**G**oddammit, them wild horses broke through our fence again." The angry man threw his hat on the ground, swore as he kicked the tire on his jeep, then snatched up the hat and beat the dust off it against the thigh of his jeans. "That's the third time this month. Dammit, that water hole is on our land, and it's for our cattle, not a bunch of wild mustangs."

His companion reached for his arm as he pulled the rifle from the back seat. "Bill, what're you doing?"

"I'm done with this crap, Mona, and I'm tired of mending this damn fence. I'm gonna put a stop to it right now."

"How do you expect to find that herd on foot?"

"There's a piece of that wire missing, and there's blood on the ground. I'd say one of them got hooked up in the wire. With any luck at all it'll be that friggin' stallion. Bring them field glasses and come on." Unhappy about it, she pulled out the binoculars and hurried after him.

NOT TOO FAR AWAY, SOMEBODY else had already found the horses. The lead stallion was down, tangled in the barbed wire, the rest of the herd had moved off a way, enjoying the warm sun and the lush grass. "Derek, you be careful, that stallion could take you apart in a heartbeat."

"I know, Jill, but he's caught up in that wire, hobbled himself, and he's bleeding. We've got to get him loose."

"Derek, no. Look, we need the others. You stay here, and I'll go for help. Please don't do anything foolish. Wait here, keep an eye on him until I get back with the others."

"All right, but make it quick." Without another word, she wheeled her horse and rode away, the wild horses parting to give her plenty of room.

As soon as she disappeared from sight, he dismounted and began to slowly approach the stallion, cooing softly to the injured animal. "Easy now, Big Red, easy now. You're all tangled up there. I'll bet that hurts. Easy now, just be still and I'll get that wire off you."

Up on the ridge someone else had found the man and the horses. He settled down and began to take careful aim. "Bill, for Christ's sake, what the hell are you doing?"

"Hush now, Mona. I'm gonna kill two birds with one stone."

"You're going to shoot him? Jesus, Bill ..."

"No, I'm not going to shoot him, for god's sake. See that big green rock beside the stallion? I'm gonna hit that. The damn horse will kick the shit out of that fool and try to run away. That'll give me a clear shot at it. That jackass'll get beat up, the stallion will be coyote meat, and no one'll ever know for sure what happened."

"Bill, don't do this, this's plain crazy."

"Just shut the hell up and watch through them field glasses. Tell me when he gets close enough to the horse."

Down on the grassland, Derek Wheeler was moving closer to the trapped animal. "Easy now, Big Red, easy." His pulse was racing, for he knew how dangerous a wild mustang could be if cornered and frightened. "Easy now." This horse was caught and definitely frightened, its eyes rolled back in terror.

He eased closer and extended his hand toward the horse's injured leg. The stallion screamed and lunged at him just as a shot rang out and the small boulder beside them exploded.

"Jesus Christ, Bill, what happened?"

"I don't know. Never seen anything like that before."

She was dragging at his arm. "Come on, we have to get the hell out of here. That man's surely dead; nobody could survive that. Hurry, we've got to get gone before somebody sees us and reports it to the police. We'll be charged with murder. Come on."

It sank into his shocked brain that she was right, and he hurried after her. Throwing the rifle in the back seat, he leaped behind the wheel and drove swiftly away.

An hour later the young woman returned with several more riders, but the stallion was gone and so was her boyfriend. There was nothing but a fine layer of green dust where the horse had lain. His horse was quietly grazing with the wild herd.

Jillian Arbend called and called, she tried his phone and heard it ringing. It was on the ground with the rest of his clothes, covered in the green dust. "What the hell?" She dismounted and picked up the shirt and jeans, shaking the dust off them.

"What is it, Jill?"

"Derek's clothes, his phone, even his boots are here, but there's no sign of him or the stallion. I don't get it. Even if he managed to free the horse, why would he strip off to ride it, as if that horse would let him. Where did he go? Why naked, and where the hell is the horse?"

"That looks like him coming there," said one of the other riders.

Jillian looked up to see the stallion on the top of the ridge, silhouetted against the setting sun. The horse bugled a call and the herd turned as one to go to him. As the herd of mustangs crossed over the ridge, the red stallion trotted down to where the riders sat atop their horses.

Slowly, cautiously, he approached Jillian. She reached out her hand and, tentatively, he approached, stretching out his neck so he could sniff at her. For just a moment he put his soft muzzle into her palm then snorted and raced away to join the herd. Almost in shock, she stood and watched as he disappeared over the ridge.

"Jill, what the hell just happened? Nobody's been able to get within a hundred yards of that horse before. He almost acted as though he knew you."

"I don't know, Merle. I really don't. What I do know is I have to find Derek. Let's spread out and start looking."

"He ain't here, Jill," said another rider. "Sun's going down, we'll find nothing today. We need to go back, report this to the sheriff, and get back here at first light with a real search party."

"Peggy's right, Jill," said Merle. "Let's get back now and set up for a proper search in the morning." Peggy and Merle were like family. Jillian sighed and allowed them to lead her away.

THE SHERIFF JUST SHOOK his head as he listened to the people explain about the disappearance of Derek Wheeler. Had it just been one of them he might have laughed it off as them smoking too much weed, but he knew several of these folks. None of it made any sense, but he believed them.

"All right, Merle, I'll make some calls, set up a search party for tomorrow. First, though, I want to have a hard look at the place where you say you found his clothes. If this is some kind of joke, or prank, I warn you, I have no sense of humor at all."

"It's not a joke, Sheriff," declared Jill. "The horse was down, tangled up in a length of barbed wire. We agreed that Derek would keep watch while I went for help. I know him too well. He's tried to set that horse free all by himself, and something went horribly wrong."

"Like what?"

"Sheriff, I have no idea at all. None. All I know is, he's gone, his clothes were left behind, scattered around like he'd been torn out of them, and there's no sign of him anywhere."

"Was there blood at the scene?"

"Only what had been there when we first found the horse."

"And the area was covered with greenish powder?"

"That's right."

"Anything else unusual?"

"No, I don't think ... wait, there was a small boulder right by the horse. It was a greenish color, but it wasn't there when we got back."

"Greenish? Like the powder?"

"Yeah, like the rock exploded into dust. Weird. Sheriff, can't we start looking for him tonight?"

"Miss, I'm sorry, but I can't even call him a missing person for forty-eight hours, besides, I don't want that crime scene getting all trampled up."

"Crime scene?"

"Yes, ma'am, by calling it a crime scene I can legally begin a search tomorrow. I follow the rules, check it out, then we start the search. It's that or wait out the forty-eight hours."

Jill gazed at him incredulously with huge eyes. "All right, Sheriff, crime scene it is." She turned and walked out of his office.

"Jill, wait," called Peggy, as she followed her out the door.

The emotion and frustration suddenly boiled over and Jillian fairly fell into Peggy's arms. "Oh, Peg, what am I going to do? Derek could be hurt, lost, ..."

"Easy, honey, easy. We'll find him. First thing we can see daylight, we'll be on horseback, looking for him. If he's out there, we'll find him. Honey, you go home and get some sleep, you're exhausted. We'll pick you up first thing in the morning." Jillian sniffed, kissed Peggy's cheek, then stepped back and turned away to Derek's old truck. Somehow she managed to fend off the tears until she got back home.

Don't miss out!

Visit the website below and you can sign up to receive emails whenever Prudence MacLeod publishes a new book. There's no charge and no obligation.

https://books2read.com/r/B-A-ZKBBB-URQYC

BOOKS 2 READ

Connecting independent readers to independent writers.

Also by Prudence MacLeod

Children of the Goddess
Lady Blue
Fallen Angel
Lady Justice
Lady Shadow
Lady Seeker
Watcher and Warrior
Shadow Ascending

Children of the Wild
Immortal Tigress
Children of the Wolf
Vampire's Lair
The Hawk and the Wolf
The Oregon Incident

Forgotten Worlds
Suvi
Echo of the Past
Survivors

Ship
Fleet
Unite
IGEN
T.E.N.

Nova series
Novan Witch
Assassin of Nova
Beyond Nova
Claimstake
Red Nova

Watch for more at https://www.prudencemacleod.com/.

Telling a story is like knitting a sweater. Start with a ball of possibilities, pull out one small thread and begin. With luck and patience you will create something quite wonderful.

About the Author

On a far off windswept island Jennifer Crandall sits with her dogs and cats creating fantastic stories for all to enjoy. She publishes as JL Crandall, Prudence MacLeod, and Jenni Leigh.

Read more at https://www.prudencemacleod.com/.